'Oh, roses — h

'I asked my housel
for you,' he tol
gesture seemed suddenly very foolish and yet
he was glad it had given her pleasure. 'If
there's anything you need, just come over and
shout.'

She turned towards him, her beautiful eyes
softened by the smile, and his fingers ached to
free her hair from the ponytail and spread it
over her shoulders. It would be like golden
rain, fanned over his pillow—— He yanked
himself up short. No, Pendragon. Not this
one.

Dear Reader

Autumn books to warm the heart! Gideon really believes he has NOTHING LEFT TO GIVE until Beth proves him wrong, in Caroline Anderson's latest story. Their past relationship makes Alison and Grant decide to be STRICTLY PROFESSIONAL in work, according to Laura MacDonald. Abigail Gordon's CALMER WATERS and Judith Ansell's HIS SHELTERING ARMS are equally touching. We think you'll love these stories.

The Editor

!!!STOP PRESS!!! If you enjoy reading these medical books, have you ever thought of writing one? We are always looking for new writers for LOVE ON CALL, and want to hear from you. Send for the guidelines, with SAE, and start writing!

Caroline Anderson's nursing career was brought to an abrupt halt by a back injury, but her interest in medical things led her to work first as a medical secretary, and then after completing her teacher training, as a lecturer in Medical Office Practice to trainee medical secretaries. In addition to writing, she also runs her own business from her home in rural Suffolk, where she lives with her husband, two daughters, mother and assorted animals.

Recent titles by the same author:

ROLE PLAY
A MAN OF HONOUR
PICKING UP THE PIECES
SECOND THOUGHTS

NOTHING LEFT TO GIVE

BY

CAROLINE ANDERSON

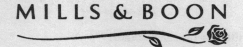

MILLS & BOON

MILLS & BOON LIMITED
ETON HOUSE, 18–24 PARADISE ROAD
RICHMOND, SURREY, TW9 1SR

All the characters in this book have no existence outside the imagination of the Author, and have no relation whatsoever to anyone bearing the same name or names. They are not even distantly inspired by any individual known or unknown to the Author, and all the incidents are pure invention.

First published in Great Britain 1994
by Mills & Boon Limited

© Caroline Anderson 1994

Australian copyright 1994   Philippine copyright 1994
This edition 1994

ISBN 0 263 78827 X

Set in 10 on 12 pt Linotron Times
03-9410-51027

Typeset in Great Britain by Centracet, Cambridge
Made and printed in Great Britain

CHAPTER ONE

THE surgery was modern, purpose-built and a huge improvement on her last place of work. Instead of a tatty, litter-strewn pavement and a door straight off the street, the path from the car park to the entrance led through a landscaped garden filled with carefully tended roses, and the air was heavy with their scent.

In the distance Beth could hear farm machinery — haymaking? Probably not; it was the middle of September. Harvesting, then? She didn't even know that much about the countryside, and yet here she was, in Barnham Market in Suffolk, about to be interviewed for a part-time temporary job that she wasn't even sure she wanted.

She stifled a disbelieving laugh. She didn't really know what she was doing there at all — except that she had no job now, and this would at least give her the chance to find out if she liked living in the country, by no means a foregone conclusion since she had never done it before.

In fact her total contact with the country consisted of a few picnics in the company of a load of townies who knew no more about it than she did!

She sighed and locked the car. Oh, well, she was here now; she might as well have the interview.

The interior of the practice was light, airy and filled with plants, a far cry from the last place with its dreary rooms and scuffed lino floors. Here, rich blue-grey

5

carpet tiles covered the floor in the reception area, and the chairs looked comfortable, grouped around a big table stacked neatly with magazines from *Country Living* to *Farmer's Weekly*. There were two women sitting in the waiting-room, both obviously pregnant, and a toddler under a table chattering happily to a big yellow teapot. There was probably an ante-natal clinic going on.

She went up to the glass hatch into the reception office and smiled at the pretty middle-aged receptionist. 'Hello, I'm Beth Turner — I've got an interview at three with Dr Pendragon.'

'Oh, yes — take a seat, would you? Dr Pendragon will be back in a minute — he's just had to go out on a call. He shouldn't be long. The nurse'll be free soon.'

She went obediently and sat down, among the pregnant women and the scattered toys, and pondered her fate.

Could be worse, she thought as she eyed the child. London had been, after all. Nothing, but nothing could be worse than that — the incessant traffic, the noise, the smell — really, she thought, you'd imagine you'd get used to it after all these years, but no. Not her, at any rate. She still loathed the noises, and as for the traffic fumes ——

'Read.'

She blinked. The toddler pushed the book into her hand, climbed on to her lap and waited expectantly, his grubby cherub's face turned up to hers. A familiar pang shot through her, but she ruthlessly ignored it.

'No, darling ——'

She turned to the mother. 'It's all right — really. I don't mind.'

'Are you sure?'

She nodded, and the little boy pushed the book at her again. 'Read!'

'Say please.'

'Peese.'

She dredged up a smile and opened the book. 'Once upon a time, there was a little boy called Thomas——'

'Me Thomas.'

She looked at him. 'Are you? Isn't that funny, both of you called Thomas!'

He plopped his thumb in his mouth and nodded, snuggling back down against her, and she turned back to the text again. She was barely started when a nurse appeared at her elbow.

'Miss Turner? I'm Julie Rudd, the practice nurse. Would you like to come through to my room and we can have a chat?'

Beth slid the reluctant Thomas to the floor, handed him the book and followed her through the big double doors into the corridor outside the surgeries. 'Sorry Dr Pendragon's still out — he's usually very reliable, but things don't always go according to plan.'

Beth nearly laughed. If things had gone according to plan, she wouldn't be here now. She smiled her understanding.

'Cup of tea?'

'Thank you, that would be lovely.'

'We may as well go in Gideon's office — he'll be back any time now, I expect. Never mind, perhaps we can get started without him. Here, take a seat for a second, I've put the kettle on.'

While she waited for Julie to return, Beth looked round. You could tell a lot about a man from his office, she'd discovered, and Gideon Pendragon was no exception. For one thing he didn't try and hide his family, she thought with a little twist of almost-forgotten pain. There were pictures on the desk—a boy in his late teens, dark, strikingly good-looking; a girl of about twelve, with the same fine dark looks and superb bone-structure; and a little girl, only three or so, with a moppet of fluffy blonde curls and brilliant blue eyes above a cherub's smile.

'Lovely kids.'

Beth jumped and turned. She had been miles away, in London with Matthew and the family he had denied.

'Yes—yes, they are.'

She took the cup of tea and sat back in the chair, preparing to be grilled. It didn't happen. Julie asked a few very general questions, flicked through her application and smiled.

'I can't think why you want to work here, but as far as I'm concerned you're heaven-sent,' she told Beth. 'Since Stephanie left last week I've been rushed off my feet, and you're available now, aren't you?'

Beth nodded. 'Yes, I am.'

'Good. That's brilliant. When Gideon comes in I'll tell him to rubber-stamp you.' She laughed and stood up. 'Will you excuse me? I've got an asthma clinic at four and I really ought to go and prepare some worksheets for the group. He won't be long—help yourself to more tea.'

She went, pulling the door to behind her, and left Beth alone in the surgery. She didn't have more tea. For some reason she discovered she was nervous, and another cup would have sat heavily on her butterflies.

Perhaps I should, she thought with a soft laugh. Maybe it would drown them.

She looked at the photos again, picking up the one of the baby and tracing the froth of curls thoughtfully with a neat, pink-tipped finger.

Gideon, she thought, rolling the name round on her tongue, tasting it. Gideon Pendragon. Unusual name. A mixture of old Cornish and American mid-west, hard, reliable, yet with a dash of excitement.

She gave a snort of laughter. He was probably short, fat and balding!

He was also late.

She put the photo down and paced across to the window. She was getting irritated. Couldn't someone else have gone out on the call for him? It really wasn't good enough. It was nearly four o'clock already!

Oh, well, look on the bright side, she thought; by the time you get back to London the rush-hour will be over.

She heard his voice first, low, deep, a reassuring rumble in the corridor.

There was a muttered expletive, then firm footsteps striding towards the door.

'Miss Turner? I do apologise.'

She stood up. He was big. It wasn't just height, although he was certainly tall enough, but there was a solidity, a substance about him that was more than physical. It was deeper than that, something that shouted dependability and inner strength, reliability and utter trustworthiness.

He thrust out his hand — large, square, of a piece with the man himself.

'I'm sorry to keep you — Gideon Pendragon.'

She placed her hand in his and felt it engulfed in a warm and reassuring grip.

'Beth Turner,' she replied, and looked up into his face.

Her smile faltered. It was a striking face, an older version of the boy in the photograph, but it was his eyes that stopped her in her tracks.

Grey-green in colour, they were beautiful, bracketed by wickedly long black lashes. They were also the oldest, most world-weary eyes she had ever seen. Her soft heart reached out to him.

'Problems?' she said gently.

'You could say that.' He gave a short laugh and thrust strong fingers through the unruly strands of his straight, black hair. 'People never die at a convenient time, do they?'

If she hadn't seen the eyes, she might have dismissed him as callous. As it was she gave him time to pull himself back into the present and pick up her file. He flicked through it and tossed it back on the desk, dropping into the chair and leaning back, his hands locked behind his head.

'So, what did Julie say? She's usually pretty direct.'

Beth's mouth twitched. 'She said she'd tell you to rubber-stamp it.'

He smiled then, and his harsh features softened, bringing life to those tired eyes. 'Good. I only had one real question.'

'Why a part-time temporary job in the middle of nowhere?'

He grinned. 'You were expecting it.'

'Sort of.' She returned the grin. 'Because I need to work, but not necessarily flat out for a while. Because I could do with a breathing-space, time to find out what I really want from my career. Because I was ready for a change, and there didn't seem to be a full-time permanent job that said, "Take me," written all over it.'

He eyed her thoughtfully. 'Why did you need a breathing space?'

She looked away. He saw too much with those eyes. 'Let's just say there was a conflict of interests.'

'A man?'

'Yes.' She didn't enlarge on it. The details were sordid and irrelevant.

'So, you're running away.'

'No.' She met his eyes again, determined to get the general principle straight, if not the fine print. 'I don't run away, Dr Pendragon. Not from anything. I simply decided it was time to move on.'

He chuckled. 'Touché. So, you're looking for a bolt-hole to lick your wounds while you decide what you want from life. Well, I won't pretend we aren't glad to have you, Miss Turner. Stephanie, our part-timer, has had to stop work rather earlier in her pregnancy than she'd planned, and we're up a gum tree. You're like a gift from the gods, frankly, and we aren't in a position to be choosy about people's reasons for wanting to take the job. Nurses of your calibre simply aren't interested, so whatever your motives, welcome.'

That was it. She had the job. Stunned, she reached over the desk and took his outstretched hand. A slow smile touched his lips. 'When can you start?'

She gave an expressive little shrug. 'Whenever— Monday?'

'Tomorrow?'

'Tomorrow?' She hesitated, totally taken aback. 'Well, I suppose I could—I haven't got anywhere to live, and I've got nothing here. I'd have to go back to London tonight and get some things to tide me over till the weekend, but I suppose I could put up in a hotel or something.'

'I've got a flat — over the old coach house. It's just one room and a bathroom. The idea was that William would have it once he goes away to college next year so it wouldn't be for very long, but as the job's only temporary I don't suppose that would matter. It's got heating and everything — do you want to have a look?'

She nodded, swept along by the current.

'Yes — why not? It sounds ideal.'

'Good — shall we?'

He held the door for her, then led her down the corridor to Reception. 'I'm just taking Miss Turner home to show her the flat — I won't be long. Oh, and stick her on the payroll, Molly — she's starting tomorrow.'

And that was it. Bemused, Beth followed him out of the side door and round into the street. The surgery was just off the market square that dominated the centre of the little town, and they walked along one side of the square and down a narrow little lane that cut through between the houses. They passed the church, built of brick and flint, solid and homely, and then beyond the church they came to a large Georgian house, the mellow cream of old Suffolk bricks, standing four-square in a neatly tended lawn.

'What a lovely house,' Beth remarked. 'Very des-res.'

He laughed softly. 'I'm glad you like it — sometimes I forget how lucky I am.'

'It's yours? I thought it was the vicarage.'

'It was — until about twenty years ago. The present incumbent lives over there, much more economically!'

He pointed to a very pleasant modern house, much more modest than the sprawling Georgian building Beth had admired. She looked back at Gideon's house, large and imposing. It suited him.

He turned in through a pair of tall gates and paused by a big brick building, itself larger than the present vicarage. Huge white-painted doors were set in the lower half, and the upper storey had tall arched windows set in the gables and dormers along the roofline. 'There you are — that's the coach house. We use the bottom as a garage. When the kids were younger they used to play in the flat, but they've outgrown that sort of thing now.'

He sounded regretful, as if their childhood had been a thing of delight for him, and she felt herself warming to him even more. What a lovely, solid, dependable family man he was — such a contrast to the fickle and faithless Matthew.

She dragged her mind back to her surroundings, refusing to waste her mental energy on such a worthless topic.

He was opening a door at the side of the coach house, and she followed him in. There was a hall which reached the full height, and above she could see the old beams stretching across the vaulted ceiling. A black cast-iron spiral staircase led upwards, its lacy treads ringing under her feet as she ran lightly up to the top.

It was wonderful — huge, light and airy, the arched windows at each end looking out over the garden on one side and fields on the other. The crop hadn't yet been harvested and the tall stalks whispered as the light breeze flowed over them. Nearer to hand she could hear the rustling of the leaves on the trees which edged the garden, and in one of the trees a bird sang, the notes pure and clear. Beth closed her eyes, speechless.

'I know the furniture's a bit old-fashioned, but it's solid and everything's quite clean. If you wanted we could get something else, I suppose — the mattress is new.'

She opened her eyes and looked around, taking in the contents of the room instead of just its atmosphere.

The walls were white, the carpet a soft, faded brick colour, and everything else blended — the warm old pine of the table and chairs, the heavily carved bed-ends, the natural oak of the beams that spanned the ceiling, and on the comfy old sofa a faded chintz cover in soft peaches and greens. At the far end was a small run of handbuilt pine units housing a little oven, a fridge and a sink unit, and on the other side a door led presumably to the bathroom.

She turned to him, a silly smile lurking on her face. 'It's perfect,' she told him, 'absolutely perfect. I can't believe my luck.'

He smiled then, the weary eyes warming, and Beth felt somthing quiver deep inside her.

'I'm glad you like it,' he said softly, and she was suddenly aware of him, of his size, his nearness in the room that was suddenly far, far too small.

She turned away, flustered. 'It's very homely — your wife must have quite a gift,' she said, deliberately reminding herself that he was married.

The silence was deafening, and something about its quality made her turn and look searchingly at him.

The weariness was back, and with it a bone-deep sadness.

'My wife's dead, Miss Turner. She's been dead for four years.'

Sophie was refusing to co-operate in the way only a four-year-old could. Gideon hung on to his patience, determined to win the battle, if not the war.

In the end she was bathed and into bed, and Claire had finished her Latin homework and was wrestling with biology. Will was in his room, Dire Straits tearing hell out of the walls and making the windows rattle. He opened the door.

'William!' he yelled.

The music was cut drastically.

'Hi, Dad.'

'Just going over to the coach house for a minute — the nurse will be here soon and I want to make sure everything's ready. Watch the girls for me, can you?'

Will did the thumbs-up, and Gideon shut the door on the awful noise and headed for the relative sanctuary of the coach house.

To be honest, he was still trying to work out why he had let her have it. It was his retreat, the oasis of tranquillity he escaped to whenever things got too much and he needed time out from the pressing reality of life as a single parent.

He closed the door behind him and sighed, letting the absolute peace and stillness soak into him.

He must be mad to give it away.

He climbed the stairs and made his way over to the kitchen area, checking that his housekeeper had put a supply of fresh food in the fridge as he had requested, and that the bed was made up and aired and the bathroom in readiness.

On impulse he went back down and picked some roses from beside the house and took them in, standing them in a glass for want of a vase. They were hardly arranged — that sort of thing wasn't his forte, to say the least, but he wanted to make the gesture — perhaps of atonement?

He had been rather abrupt, but he really hadn't wanted to get into a discussion of Denise's death and the events surrounding it.

He set the roses down on the table and dropped into the sofa, stretching his legs out in front of him and dropping his head back with a sigh.

Damn, she was pretty.

Soft and warm, like sunshine on a spring morning.

He snorted. Poetry now.

He was conscious of an ache, deep in his chest, and another tightness further down, an awareness, a need that had lain dormant for years.

No, he told himself. She was too sweet, too kind, too innocent to use for the slaking of his thirst.

Hell, she wouldn't even know the rules.

A car scrunched gravel on the drive, and he went down and opened the door.

She was climbing out of the car and dragging a heavy case behind her. Chivalry bade him take it from her.

'Anything else?'

Her sweet fragrance drifted against his skin, and the ache intensified.

'No, that's all for now. I'll go back at the weekend.'

He turned without speaking and went back inside, carrying the heavy case ahead of him up the steps.

He set it beside the bed and dusted off his hands.

'Oh, roses — how thoughtful,' she said softly, and he felt colour brush his neck.

'I asked my housekeeper to get the room ready for you,' he told her. The romantic little gesture seemed suddenly very foolish, and yet he was glad it had given her pleasure.

The huge room suddenly seemed suffocatingly small.

'Right, I'll leave you to get settled in. If there's anything you need, just come over and shout.'

She turned towards him, her beautiful blue eyes softened by the smile, and his fingers ached to free her hair from the ponytail and spread it over her shoulders. He could almost feel the silky strands sliding through his fingers. It would be like golden rain, fanned over his pillow, cascading across his chest as she raised herself to look down on him, a teasing smile on her lips ——

He yanked himself up short. No, Pendragon. Not this one.

He bade her goodnight and turned, running quickly down the stairs and out into the blessed darkness of the night.

Gideon — Beth found it impossible to think of him as Dr Pendragon — tracked her down the following morning at the surgery.

'All right?' he asked.

She nodded. 'Fine, thanks. I think I can find everything I'll need. I'm helping Julie get rid of the backlog and then I'll start my proper routine from Monday.'

'Good. Make sure you put in a claim for the extra hours. Oh, by the way, talking about extra hours, do you feel happy about taking over the Stop Smoking clinic? I forgot to mention it at your interview. We run it when necessary, and we had a new group scheduled to start on Monday evening.'

She shook her head. 'No problem. I've run one before. Do you do much with it?'

'Oh, yes, it's a tandem effort. We've found it's very cost-effective because the smokers take up so much of our time and resources, especially in the winter months. It's just that I've got a man coming to see me this morning who's been referred for bypass surgery and he's a heavy smoker — he needs to give up, and the surgeon is being less than hopeful about his chances if he doesn't, so I thought I'd talk him into the clinic.'

'Good idea.'

'Sure you don't mind? I'm sorry I didn't mention it yesterday.'

'It doesn't matter. I think I'm going to find the time hangs on my hands anyway, I'm used to being busy.'

For a moment she thought he was going to say something else, but then he nodded and turned briskly away.

Beth watched him go, the long, lazy stride eating up the ground, the supple movements of his shoulders, the swing of his arms, his movements all graceful and co-ordinated like a natural athlete.

She had heard gravel scrunch underfoot this morning outside the coach house and had watched as he jogged down the lane past the church and out into the square.

Half an hour later she had heard the scrunch of returning footsteps, and had forced herself to ignore them and not look, however tempted she might be by the long, sleek limbs spangled with dark hair, the breadth of those powerful shoulders over neat, narrow hips and the driving pistons of his legs. One look was enough. After all, she had her sanity to consider, and tangling with all that raw masculine energy wasn't conducive to mental health.

She busied herself in her room, doing inoculations and well-person checks, dishing out leaflets on breast and testicle self-examination, eating for health and avoiding heart disease.

One elderly lady, Mabel Robinson, came to her for a new dressing on her leg ulcer. Plopping down into the chair with a wheeze, she smiled up at Beth.

'Hello, dear. Just give me a second and I'll slip my stocking off for you.'

Beth returned the smile and knelt at her feet. 'Don't worry, I'll do it. You've got to have a dressing changed, is that right?'

'Yes—perishing leg ulcer. I don't know, the blessed thing doesn't seem to want to get better.'

'Let's have a look shall we?' Beth gently rolled the stocking down and slipped it off Mrs Robinson's foot, then after washing her hands she eased the hydrocolloid dressing away from the wound. 'Oh, yes, I see what you mean. It's obviously being a bit naughty, isn't it? Well, let's give it a wash and I'll ask Dr Pendragon to have a look at it.'

She cleaned the wound gently with saline, then rang through to Gideon's office and asked him to drop in.

He stuck his head round the door a moment later and shot Mrs Robinson a cheeky grin.

'Hello, Mabel—how're you doing?'

'Oh, you know, Doctor—up and down.'

He crouched on the floor beside Beth and bent over the ulcer, pursing his lips thoughtfully.

'Well, I think it looks better than last time, but it

certainly isn't progressing fast. Perhaps we should try some paste in it. That might help dry it up a little.'

Beth nodded, then redressed the wound, filling the pitting in the leg with Comfeel paste before replacing the colloid dressing with a fresh one. While she worked Mrs Robinson quizzed her openly.

'You're new, aren't you?'

Beth nodded. 'Yes, that's right. It's my first day.'

'Staying with Dr Pendragon, I hear.'

'In the coach house flat,' Beth filled in hastily. No point in letting that rumour run away with itself! But it seemed her patient was better informed than that.

'Oh, I know that, dear,' she said. 'Wonderful now, isn't it? Met the children yet?'

Beth shook her head. 'No — no, I haven't.

'Lovely children — such a shame about the mother.'

'Mmm.' Beth was deliberately non-committal, not wishing to get into a discussion about Gideon with this sweet but congenitally nosy old dear — and particularly not about his wife. She had already floundered in there where angels with any sense would fear to tread. 'How does that feel?' she asked.

'Better. Thank you so much, dear.'

Beth showed her out, holding the door for the fragile little woman, and as she watched her go she wondered how far the old lady had to come.

'Mrs Robinson?' she called, running after her. 'Would it help you if the district nurse came to do your dressing?'

Bright eyes sparkled up at Beth. 'Oh, no, dear — I'd miss all the gossip! Besides, I only live next door.'

Beth smiled and let her go. The exercise and change of scene was probably good for her, anyway.

David Hendry, Gideon's smoking heart bypass patient, walked past her as she was about to go back in. She knew it was him because as he passed her he paused to speak, then raised his hand to his mouth and coughed, and Beth could hear the damage he was doing in the bronchitic rattle from his chest.

'Nasty cough you've got there,' she said conversationally. 'Bad cold?'

'Nah — damn fags cause that. The dreaded weed.'

She smiled sympathetically. 'Tough giving up, isn't it? I used to smoke myself when I was training, but I gave up when I became a staff nurse! I still remember how hard it was.'

Her patient snorted. 'You're telling me. I've tried — God knows I've tried, but this time it's got to work. There's just too much at stake.' He met her eyes, his own pleading. 'I gather you're running the Stop Smoking clinic with Dr Pendragon.'

'That's right.'

His mouth twisted. 'Well, I wish you luck with me. I can't do it on my own, but I really must make it stick this time.'

She laid a hand on his shoulder and smiled. 'We'll get you there, Mr Hendry, don't you worry. You'll do it this time. I won't let you fail.'

He met her eyes, and she could see doubt and scepticism mingled with hope in their depths.

'I'll see you Monday, then.'

She watched him go, a relatively young man whom lack of exercise, family history and years of self-abuse had threatened with an untimely end. Could she save him? Not alone, of course, but would her contribution make any difference to the final outcome?

She didn't know, but one thing she was sure of — she'd have a damn good try.

Friday, and the end of the week. Beth dropped the patient records back into Reception and smiled at Molly.

'All done?'

She nodded. 'I hope so. I've got to sort some things out for the Stop Smoking clinic on Monday, but otherwise I think I've done everything.'

'Good.' Molly glanced up at her. 'Settling in all right at the Rectory?'

'Oh, yes — it's lovely,' Beth told her honestly, genuinely delighted by her accommodation. She was less sure about her boss, though. Other than strictly professional exchanges, he had been very distant since the first night — really, since she had made that remark about his wife.

How was she to know, though? The man didn't have a brand on his forehead that proclaimed him a widower. She felt bad that she'd hurt him, even so, especially after he had bent over backwards to make her welcome.

His desperation had certainly been justified, she acknowledged. She had worked full-time these past two days to help Julie catch up with her backlog, and then from Monday would be working just the mornings and Tuesday afternoon, as planned, with the smoking cessation clinic on Monday evenings some of the time.

For someone used to working full-time, it wasn't much. She would have to find something to fill her leisure hours. Maybe one of her elderly patients had a dog that needed walking, or perhaps she could do some shopping for one of them. She'd ask — but not now. Now, she wanted to find a shop in the square and buy something to eat tonight, and then go back and cook it and eat it in front of the television, curled up on that unbelievably comfortable sofa.

Maybe she'd take up patchwork or tapestry or something to while away the long winter evenings.

It was only September, but already the nights were drawing in and there was a chill in the air.

She said goodnight to Molly and headed for the door.

Spaghetti, perhaps, or maybe a couple of those wonderful cheeses from the specialist food shop that lurked innocently on one side of the square.

She went in and bought some dolcelatte and a slice of a sheep's milk roulé, and then on impulse picked up a bottle of Chianti.

'Celebrating something?'

He didn't mean to speak to her, but it was difficult to avoid her all the time and he didn't want to be conspicuously churlish.

She turned and smiled, the wine in her hand. 'Not really — it just looked appealing.'

'You shouldn't drink alone,' he found himself saying.

She shrugged. 'I don't, as a rule, but — well, I thought tonight. . .'

She looked suddenly wistful, and he found himself asking her to join them for supper. 'Nothing fancy — just spaghetti bolognese, I think, tonight. It's Will's turn, and he always does spaghetti.'

She nearly laughed. 'I was going to cook that for myself.'

'So will you come?' He found himself waiting for her reply.

'Thank you, yes, I will. I'll bring the cheeses — we can have them afterwards.'

Her smile brushed her eyes with gold, and he felt the ache start again, low down. Damn. Now what had he done?

'Fine,' he said tersely. 'Seven o'clock?'

'That would be lovely — if you're sure?'

'Quite sure,' he lied. 'We'll see you then — I'll leave the lights on.'

CHAPTER TWO

IN FACT it was still fairly light at seven o'clock although dusk was creeping in, but the lights made the big house seem even more welcoming as Beth scrunched up the gravel drive and rang the doorbell.

She waited for a moment, then rang it again. She could hardly hear it in the distance, over the music — at least two sorts, if not three — and the screaming of a child.

She smiled. That would be the small girl, in a paddy if she was any judge. She opened the door and walked into a scene of utter pandemonium.

The little girl was lying on the floor screaming, there was steam billowing out of the kitchen, and from the depths of the steam something with a heavy bass-line throbbed and wailed at full blast. The television was blaring forth from another room, and something else filtered down from upstairs.

She closed her eyes and tried not to laugh. Poor man, no wonder he hadn't heard the doorbell!

She went into the kitchen and found it empty except for a pan of boiling water and the music. Both needed switching off — she went for the music first. Then she found the TV in the breakfast-room next door and switched that off.

The silence was shattering. Even the little girl stopped screaming to listen to it.

She went back out into the hall, now quiet except for the music emanating from an upstairs room.

'Hello,' she said to the child, and she sat up and eyed Beth warily.

''lo.'

'I'm Beth.'

'I'm Sophie.'

She sat on the floor beside the child. 'What's wrong, Sophie?'

'Nothing,' she mumbled mutinously. 'I can't find Daddy. I called him.'

Beth shot a glance at the kitchen. 'I don't suppose he could hear you. Shall we see if we can find him?'

'Who turned that off?' a voice yelled over the banisters, and a youth vaulted over the top rail on to the middle of the first flight and bounded down to the hall.

'I did.'

'Ah.' He skidded to a halt at her feet and peered down at her. 'Um — is Sophie all right?'

She looked up at a younger version of Gideon, thinner and still a little gangly, but filling out fast. The eyes were identical.

'I think so — I imagine she was just trying to make herself heard,' she said drily.

He flushed. 'You must be the nurse.' He held down his hand and hauled her to her feet with a grin. 'I'm William.'

She returned the grin. 'I'm Beth. I turned off your hot water, as well, but there wasn't much left.'

There was a tug at her hand. 'Find Daddy,' Sophie demanded.

William scooped her up into his arms. 'Daddy's in the shower.' He looked over Sophie to Beth. 'He sends his apologies — he won't be a sec. He's had a bit of a crisis in the bathroom. You couldn't help me get Sophie into bed so I can get the spaghetti on, could you? The sauce is made.'

'I want 'ghetti.'

'You've had yours — go on, Tuppence, don't be a pain.' He kissed her and handed her over to Beth. 'Top of the stairs, turn sharp right. You can't miss her room — it's got pink furry things all over the floor.'

Sophie giggled. 'He means My Little Ponies. Want to see?'

Beth smiled at her, her heart twisting. She was such a cherub. 'Love to. Shall we?'

She set her down and they walked together up the stairs, hand in hand, while Beth wondered what sort of a crisis Gideon could possibly have had in the bathroom. She didn't have to wonder for long.

'I had a bath,' Sophie told Beth seriously as they mounted the stairs. 'A big one.'

'Oh,' Beth replied just as seriously. 'Very big?'

Sophie nodded. 'Too big — all the water fell over the top, and all the bubbles. Daddy threw a mega.'

She caught the laugh just in time. That expression just had to be straight out of her big brother's or sister's mouth. Lips twitching, she turned the corner at the top of the stairs just in time to see Gideon cross the landing clad only in a towelling robe belted loosely on his hips.

'Beth!'

She smiled uncertainly. 'Um — Sophie was yelling for you. William asked me to put her to bed. . .'

'That boy — OK, Tuppence, come on, let's tuck you up — '

She hid her hands firmly behind her back.

'Beth do it.'

'No, Daddy do it — '

'No.' The chin stuck out, the cherub lips pursed in a determined little pout.

'Really, I don't mind——'

'Sophie——'

'Please, Daddy, please?'

They stood looking down at the little minx, and Beth had a sudden pang in the region of her heart that just wouldn't be denied. 'I would like to—may I? I could read her a story while you get changed.'

He glanced down, as if he had suddenly realised he was hardly dressed for the occasion, and a slow, rueful smile crawled across his face.

'Be my guest,' he said gruffly, and turned away from her. 'Ten minutes, Sophie, all right?'

'All right,' she piped, and, taking Beth's hand, she led her into her room.

It was a lovely evening. Claire, the middle child, was quiet and watchful at first, but having established Beth was not a threat she opened up and was quite charming. Will was good fun, Beth decided, despite the shatteringly loud music, and Sophie—well, she had fallen in love with Sophie sitting on the hall floor and nothing had happened to change that. Gideon was a bit of an enigma, though, quiet and watchful like Claire but without opening up.

Maybe he never did. The children didn't seem to think there was anything unusual in his behaviour, and he was perfectly polite. It was just that he was withdrawn, almost as if he regretted issuing the invitation, and when she said she ought to be going he leapt to his feet with alacrity.

'I'll walk you back,' he said firmly, and so she said

goodnight to the children, thanked William for cooking the meal and allowed Gideon to hustle her out of the door.

He didn't really, it was just that she was being oversensitive — or perhaps just picking up accurately on something he had meant to keep to himself.

They walked back to the coach house with only the sound of gravel underfoot to break the silence, glad now of the outside lights that dispelled the shadows of the trees and drove the spooks away.

'I'm sorry about the chaos when you arrived,' he said finally as they arrived at her door.

She shot him a wry grin. 'I should imagine it's like that in most families in the evening,' she replied, unaware of the slight wistfulness in her voice.

He tipped his head, watching her thoughtfully. 'Do you have any brothers or sisters?'

She nearly laughed. 'No,' she told him instead. 'Once was enough for my parents. I disrupted the even tenor of their peaceful academia quite sufficiently without them making a habit of it.'

'You sound bitter.'

'Do I? I'm sorry, I would have thought by now I'd got over that. I have, really. It's just — well, tonight — you're a very lucky man, Gideon. A very lucky man.'

His laugh was low and hollow. 'It doesn't always seem like that.'

'When you're mopping the bathroom floor, for instance?'

He snorted. 'Exactly. Oh, well. Thank you for your help with Sophie, by the way. She can be a real treasure when she's not arguing.'

'I noticed.'

A silence fell between them, a silence heavy with awareness and tension. He reached behind her and opened the door, pushing it wide.

'You'd better go in before you get cold,' he muttered, his voice husky.

'Thank you for a lovely evening.'

'My pleasure. Goodnight.' He turned and walked away, his footsteps crunching. She shut the door. Had he been about to kiss her?

She wouldn't like to bet on it either way, but she rather thought. . .

Nonsense. She ran up the stairs, unable to resist looking out of the window towards the house. He was standing by the door and waved before turning to go in.

Waiting for her, to see if she would look at him?

God knows, she thought. She whipped the curtains shut. Involvement with another family man was the last thing she needed right now, even if he was widowed and his tiny daughter had felt so absolutely right in her achingly empty arms. . .

She spent the weekend moving things up from London and writing endless letters changing her address. The flat was rented, so she gathered all her meagre belongings and took them to Suffolk, storing them easily in the huge cupboards in the coach house flat.

At six o'clock, just as she realised she was starving and was wondering what she could find to eat, she heard footsteps on the gravel and her doorbell rang.

She went down to find William there, lounging casually against the wall, a lazy grin on his face.

'Dad says would you like to join us for supper? He's got something he wants to ask you about. He would have come but he's had a bit of a crisis with the Yorkshire puds and Sophie's spilt the gravy all over the table.'

She controlled the smile, but apparently not well enough.

'I should get that out of your system here,' Will told her with a grin. 'He's like Queen Victoria at the moment — definitely not amused.'

She laughed. 'Poor Gideon. Yes, I'd love to join you — am I OK or should I change?'

Will ran an eye over her jeans and sweatshirt, and raised an eyebrow. 'You'll do fine. Dad's probably changed, but then he had gravy down his front, so he didn't have a choice.'

She ran back up for her keys, flicked off the lights and followed William back to the house. They went in through the back door this time, straight into the heart of the chaos.

It was a quieter sort of chaos this time, Beth realised, but still fairly hectic.

The vegetables were boiling over, and while William dealt with them Beth scooped Sophie off the worktop just as she tried to reach the top cupboard.

'I want a biscuit!' the indignant child yelled, but Beth was not impressed.

'No. It's supper-time, you'll spoil your appetite. Let's go and see if we can help Daddy.'

'He doesn't want to see me in there again until I've learned not to be a windmill,' she told Beth dolefully.

She just managed to stop her lips from twitching. 'Oh, dear. Never mind, you come with me and keep your hands down and you'll be all right.'

She went out into the hall and found Claire sitting on

the floor, the flex of the phone wound round her arm and hand, rolling her eyes. 'Well, don't do it, then! I can't believe how you let them rule your life. Tell them no, you don't want to practise — oh, Annie, what do you mean you can't?'

Beth walked past her into the dining-room just as Gideon walked out yelling to Claire to put the damn phone down.

They both slammed to a halt, nose to nose, and Gideon ran his fingers through well-tousled hair and shot her a fraught grin. 'Hi, Beth. Glad you could make it — I could do with a little sanity round here.'

She smiled back. 'Anything I can do?'

He shook his head. 'No, it's as good as it's going to get. Let's eat and forget it.'

Together they brought the last of the food through and Beth watched as he deftly slivered the rare beef and piled it on the plates.

He might have had the odd crisis *en route*, but there was nothing wrong with the end product at all — if one discounted the absence of Yorkshire puddings and the small amount of gravy that had escaped Sophie's wind-milling arms.

They all tucked in, and after it was finished and they had cleaned up a huge chocolate gâteau from the bakery in the village, Gideon sent Beth into the drawing-room while he put Sophie to bed and William and Claire cleared up the kitchen.

A few minutes later he reappeared, two mugs of coffee in his hands, and pushed the door shut behind him with his hip.

'Peace,' he said with a sigh, and dumping the coffee on the table, he dropped into the other end of the settee and smiled weakly. 'Sorry it's always so chaotic when you come round.'

'It must be very difficult coping,' she told him honestly, and he laughed.

'Oh, God, you aren't joking! Actually, that's one reason I wanted to see you. My housekeeper's not well — she's got angina, and she's been getting worse gradually over the past few months. She had a TIA, a transient ischaemic attack, like a temporary stroke, over the weekend, and I think the time's come for her to stop. And that, as you can imagine, leaves me with a problem.'

'Gosh, yes, I can imagine it does!'

His next words caught her completely by surprise.

'I don't suppose you'd consider helping out? Just a couple of hours every afternoon after Sophie comes out of school until I get back? The odd bit of shopping — I can do most of it at the weekend or one evening, but I can't expect Will or Claire to cook a meal or look after Sophie when they've got homework of their own to do. I'd pay you what I pay you at the surgery — we could offset the rent against it or something, and of course you'd eat with us.'

He fell silent, and she stared at her feet, unsure what to say.

'I'm sorry,' he mumbled into the silence. 'Of course you don't want to do it — I don't know what possessed me to ask you.'

'No — no, please — can I think about it? I mean, it wouldn't have occurred to me to look for another job, but I was wondering what I could do to fill in the time. I hate being idle — can I let you know?'

He looked relieved, she thought, that she hadn't

given him an outright refusal. She wasn't sure, in fact, why she hadn't, because she was very torn. The trouble was, she realised later as she lay in bed thinking it over, she wanted to do it too badly.

Sophie had carved a little niche in her heart, and watching Will and Claire with Gideon just made her aware of how much she had missed with her own parents.

So working for him would be very bitter-sweet.

Maybe it wouldn't be a good idea after all.

Which was ridiculous, because she had nothing better to do, and some frightful creature might end up looking after Sophie and she could become very unhappy as a result.

No, she would do it, she decided — and refuse house-room to the mocking voice that questioned her motives. Of course she wasn't doing it to be near Gideon! After all, she was near him all day at work!

But it wasn't quite the same, and in her heart she knew it.

Monday dawned bright and clear, one of those lovely late September days that made you wonder why you lit the fire the night before.

Beth dressed carefully in her uniform, made her bed and let herself out of the flat. A brisk two-minute walk was just what she needed to blow away the cobwebs.

A scrunch of gravel behind her made her turn her head in time to see Gideon coming down the drive towards her.

She waited for him, deciding to give him her decision straight away.

His smile was distracted.

'Problems?' she asked.

'Claire — she said she wasn't feeling very well and refused to go to school.'

'Oh. Well, if it helps I'll go over as soon as I finish and see how she is.'

He shot her a curious look. 'I don't suppose you've given my suggestion any further thought, have you?'

'As a matter of fact, yes — I've decided I'll do it, but only in return for the rent. I don't want to be paid — not if I'm eating with you as well, and it would make sense to do that if you're sure?'

He stopped in his tracks, turning to her, his grey-green eyes filled with relief. 'Oh, Beth, I don't know how to thank you — '

She gave a dry laugh. 'You haven't tasted my cooking yet!'

He chuckled. 'It can't be worse than Mrs Archer's.'

'Hmm. I should reserve judgement, if I were you.'

They walked the rest of the way mostly in silence, with Gideon putting in the odd comment about routine while Beth wondered if it was really going to be such a good idea spending any more time than was strictly necessary in the company of this very attractive man.

The first session of the Stop Smoking clinic was a delight for Beth. She found that she agreed wholeheartedly with everything Gideon said, and that the videos, leaflets and advice he exposed the patients to followed almost exactly the routine she had been using.

She then talked to the patients about why they wanted to give up, and what made them smoke in the first place. They were then given a diary, and asked to set a date for giving up.

'Don't think of it as giving up — that implies self-sacrifice,' Gideon told them. 'Think of it instead as taking control of your life again, instead of allowing tobacco to rule your actions. Note down in the diary when you smoke, and why. There will be some cigarettes that are harder to give up than others. Note which ones you think they will be.'

When the patients left, she could see some of them already looked discouraged.

'They always want a miracle,' Gideon said on the way home. 'They seem to think we're going to wave a wand and it will all come right. Zap! No more cravings, no more addiction, just "I'm a non-smoker". What they don't realise is that they will always be smokers now, they just won't be doing it.'

'Unless they fail,' Beth said drily.

'Oh, yes — and lots of them will. I think we'll lose at least one by next week.'

'Not David Hendry, though.'

'No — no, not Hendry. He's determined. He's already cut down from sixty to thirty. I don't know when he finds the time!'

Beth laughed. 'He needs an occupation that uses his hands — he wouldn't be able to then.'

'Huh! They just stick one in their mouths and breathe round it! It really is the biggest curse of our society, I think — worse than Hep B or HIV or alcohol, even. The trouble is it's acceptable.'

'Is it?' Beth asked. 'Not to me it isn't. I resent having to breathe other people's stale smoke.'

Gideon gave a grunt of agreement. 'The trouble is, once started it's so hard to stop. I feel sorry for them.'

'Did you notice how many of them have started smoking just by chance?' she said.

'Yes — and that's why I'm making damn sure that my kids know how dangerous and anti-social it is, because it only takes one cigarette and a lifetime's habit can be started.' He turned his head towards her. 'You did well.'

She returned the compliment, ignoring the kick of her heart against her ribs. 'So did you.'

They shared a smile, and Beth felt herself falling further into what could only be a disastrous attraction. Damn, why did she have to find him so attractive? And it wasn't just a physical thing, that was what was so dangerous. Sex appeal she could put in its proper place, but this was so much more complex, so much more insidious.

She suddenly began to wonder if sitting down at the table every evening with him and his children would actually be less harmful than starving!

Claire was on the hall floor when they went in, tangled in the phone flex as usual, lying on her back with her legs up the wall and giggling.

She looked the picture of health and fitness, and Gideon told her to get off the phone and take her feet off the wallpaper.

Beth followed him through to the kitchen, noting his scowl. 'Um — I did a casserole — the children have all had theirs.'

He looked blankly at her, then sighed. 'Sorry, I was miles away. That girl — '

' — is just like any other teenager. She's fine.'

'That,' he growled, 'is precisely my point. There's nothing at all wrong with the little skiver. I'm starving.'

Beth stifled a grin. 'Where do you want to eat?'

'In here,' he told her, and opening a cupboard, he retrieved a couple of wine glasses. 'Join me?'

'Oh — thanks, yes, I will.'

While she took the casserole out of the oven and dished up, he opened a bottle and poured the wine, then handed her a glass. He raised his to her.

'Here's celebrating my cleverness for finding such a treasure.'

She flushed and laughed uncomfortably. 'You haven't tried the food yet.'

'It smells wonderful.' His eyes were still locked with hers, and her breath lodged in her throat. She looked quickly away.

'Um — let's eat.'

'Good idea,' he said easily, and she found he was holding the chair for her in a display of old-fashioned good manners she had forgotten existed.

As he moved away his hand brushed her shoulder, and fire shot down her arm and across her back, leaving a tingling in its wake.

This was going to be next to impossible.

Beth dropped with a sigh on to the sofa in her flat, eased off her shoes and tucked her feet under her bottom. Her first full, proper week both at the surgery and as Gideon's housekeeper was over.

And she found, to her surprise, that far from being a trial it had been a pleasure. Everyone at the surgery, from Andrew Jones and Judith Wight, Gideon's partners, Julie Rudd the other nurse, Molly the receptionist and Jean Rivers the practice manager, to Mrs Horrell, the cleaner, had all been universally welcoming and friendly, and as for her other job — well!

Sophie was an angel — mostly — and Claire and Will were helpful to a point. She found the intimacy of caring for Gideon's house and family strange at first, but she soon got into the swing of it.

There was no cleaning to do, as such, because Mrs Horrell who did the surgery also did the house, and so all that Beth had to manage was the laundry, the cooking and Sophie after school.

Gideon wouldn't let her clear up after the meal, so she made sure as much as possible was loaded into the dishwasher or dealt with before he got home.

That, of course, was when her problems really started, she thought now, snuggling deeper into the sofa.

Gideon.

Tall, strong, shouldering all his responsibilities without a murmur, so grateful for her help.

She wondered how grateful he would be if he could see into her mind as she ironed his shirts and folded his underwear.

It was just playing house, helping to pass the time, she told herself, but it was more insidious than that.

She was playing his wife, and she knew it. Every time she took Sophie in her arms for a hug, or hung a shirt up in the wardrobe in his bedroom, she allowed herself to imagine that any minute he would come home and sweep her into his arms and kiss her.

That was where the danger lay. Not in anything Gideon himself had done, but in what she had allowed herself to dream.

That evening he had finished surgery earlier than

usual, and Beth was in his bedroom hanging shirts in the wardrobe when he arrived.

Well, she wasn't really hanging shirts up, rather standing with them in her arms, gazing at the huge mahogany four-poster that dominated his bedroom and trying to imagine how it would feel to lie there in his arms.

When he walked in, her eyes turned to him and she froze. He had already wrenched off his tie and undone the buttons on his shirt, and she stood transfixed, mesmerised by the broad expanse of hair-strewn chest exposed to her startled gaze.

'Sorry—I was putting away your washing,' she said weakly, and then lifted her eyes to his.

Something deep and dark shifted in them, and then he reached out his hand. 'Is that a clean shirt?'

Wordlessly she gave it to him and he laid it on the bed, stripping off the one he was wearing and tossing it at the laundry basket. He reached for his zip and she swallowed.

'Give me five minutes in the shower, could you, and I'll be down for supper.'

She mumbled something incoherent and left, picking up his shirt as she went.

Mistake. It was still warm from his body, the subtle scent of his skin lingering on the fine cotton, and she buried her nose in it and breathed deeply.

Desire, hot and sharp, darted through her leaving her weak and trembling.

Angry with herself for such foolishness, she ran downstairs, threw the shirt into the washing machine ready for the next load and got the plates out, banging them on the table.

Idiot. What did she think she was doing? He was oblivious to her — quite oblivious. She meant nothing to him except in her capacity as nurse and housekeeper.

Supper was the usual chaotic event, and Beth's quietness went unremarked. In fact had she been able to get a word in edgeways it would have been more remarkable.

As she watched Gideon in action with his children, the ache round her heart intensified. If only, she thought, but she had given up hoping long ago. Happiness would never come her way. She had always been on the outside looking in, from her childhood onwards. She had never belonged, never been wanted for herself.

Once she had thought she was truly loved, but it had been a foolish dream, and she should know better now than to indulge those dreams.

Dreams, after all, like hope, were easily shattered.

She washed up her cup and made her way to bed, snuggling under the quilt and blocking out all thoughts of Gideon. She thought instead of her job, of the people she had met and the lovely town which had made her so welcome.

Gradually she relaxed into sleep, but the dreams came then, dreams of her and Gideon and a huge old bed, of murmured sighs and soft caresses, of lightning heat and tender cries of love. . .

Gideon lay staring at the ceiling. Nothing he did would banish her. Even his shirt when he had taken it from her earlier held the lingering trace of her scent where she had held it against those small, soft breasts.

His body tautened, desire stabbing him, and he rolled on to his front, burying his face in a pillow.

Damn her. No, damn himself. She had done nothing.
She was sweet and innocent, her face transparent.

The hunger he had seen on it was echoed now in his
body, stalking his loins, making him ache for the release
only Beth could give him.

Except she couldn't, because he wouldn't let her. He
couldn't. Damn it, she was nearer to Will's age than his.
What would she want with him?

And besides, the whole idea was fruitless. Beth was a
forever person, a happy-ever-after and roses-round-the-
door sort of girl. There was neither time nor emotion
left in his life for the sort of loving she deserved.

Try telling his body that.

With a ragged groan he thumped the pillow and
turned on to his side and made an effort to relax.

Slowly sleep came, but with it dreams — dreams of
Beth, her slender limbs entwined around him, her
mouth soft and warm against his skin, her eyes luminous
with love.

He woke abruptly, his heart pounding, his body
screaming for release. Unable to sleep, unable to
tolerate the frustration and unwilling to examine the
wash of loneliness that had hit him as he realised he was
alone, he threw off the bedclothes, dragged on his
clothes and went down to the study.

If he was going to be awake, he might as well be doing
something useful.

CHAPTER THREE

MABEL ROBINSON came back on Monday to have her ulcer dressing changed. She had been instructed to return for a new dressing when the old one became transparent, and had phoned in the morning to ask if she could come in.

She had asked for Beth by name, and the feeling of pride and satisfaction that gave Beth was out of all proportion to the scale of the request.

She went into the waiting-room and smiled at her patient.

'Would you like to come through now, Mrs Robinson?'

The elderly lady eased herself to her feet and shuffled across the room to Beth, a smile flickering in her rheumy eyes.

'Morning, dear. Lovely day today.'

'Isn't it. How's the leg been?'

'Oh, well, you know, I think maybe it's a little better.'

Beth opened the door of her surgery and showed Mrs Robinson in, helping her into the chair.

'There, now, let's have a look, shall we?'

She peeled down the stocking and eased off the dressing, then washed her hands and opened the saline pack. After she had carefully cleaned the ulcer, she sat back on her heels and studied it.

Yes, it was definitely better. The necrotic edges had

been debrided by the action of the paste, and the wound was considerably cleaner than before.

'Oh, it looks quite red!' Mrs Robinson said warily, peering at the ulcer.

'That's because all the dead tissue has been absorbed by the paste and it's cleaned the skin up. It should heal much better now.'

She carefully dried the skin around the edges of the wound, filled the deeper pits with paste and firmly smoothed a new dressing over the top.

'There, that should do you until the middle of next week, I think. Keep an eye on it, though, and come back sooner if you're worried or it's uncomfy. OK?'

Mrs Robinson nodded, fastened her suspenders and got unsteadily to her feet,

'Thank you, dear, that feels lovely,' she said, and headed out of the door.

Good grief, Beth thought, I got away without a grilling on my relationship with Gideon!

She followed Mrs Robinson down the hall and was just about to open the waiting-room door when the woman craned her neck and looked up at her.

'I gather you've taken Kay Archer's job.'

Beth frowned in puzzlement. She thought the nurse had been called Stephanie.

'At Dr Pendragon's house,' Mrs Robinson continued. 'Mind you don't work too hard, my dear — that's a great big place to keep, and those children aren't the easiest, for all they're such lovely mites.'

The thought of Will being described as a lovely mite made Beth want to laugh. However, she concentrated on answering Mrs Robinson sensibly.

'Don't you worry about me — it's a pleasure working there. I love the house, and the children are fun.'

Mrs Robinson eyed her thoughtfully, and Beth had a horrible sinking feeling that the old lady was a lot more astute than she appeared.

She gave a non-committal grunt, and Beth opened the door and watched her go. Would it be all round the little town by lunchtime that Beth Turner was in love with Gideon Pendragon?

The thought hit her with a jolt.

In love? Where had that come from?

Surely not. . .

The Stop Smoking clinic that evening was the first time she had seen Gideon since after supper on Friday. As she prepared the waiting-room she wondered how she would manage to face him in the light of her new discovery.

Did it show in her eyes? She checked quickly in the mirror on the wall by the door, and noticed nothing out of the ordinary. Her blue eyes looked — well, blue, really. Nothing striking, no lightning zig-zagging across them, no neons flashing or LED lights running round her lashes!

No, it was all hidden carefully inside, and that was the way it was going to stay.

She got out the patients' cards, the leaflets and tip-sheets on diversionary tactics, and a whole host of little toys and gimmicks — stress-balls, squidgy rubbery balls that could be squeezed and squashed almost beyond recognition; chewing-gum — not nicotine gum but the ordinary sort that would help by giving the mouth a task without sustaining the need for nicotine, because some supposed ex-smokers had been reported to be still using the nicotine replacements a year later.

She also set out some nicotine patches which although they were also tobacco replacements at least gave a smaller, more sustained dose of nicotine and removed the mouth and hands from the habit, so that the level of the drug and the activities of the body became unrelated, helping to break the habit. They were easier to give up, too.

As she was setting out the last of the things Gideon appeared at her side.

'Of course none of it will work without a bit of self-control and will-power,' he said, and tossed one of the stress-balls in the air. 'I read of a GP in Essex who advocates juggling among other things — as he said, it's difficult to smoke and keep three balls in the air at the same time!'

Beth chuckled, and watched as he attempted to juggle with the balls.

They fell all around him, and she laughed aloud.

He bent to pick them up and straightened, a wry grin on his face. 'Can you do it better?'

She shook her head. 'No.'

He dropped them back on the table. 'I think the idea's of limited use, anyway. Most of these people smoke while they read or watch TV or even at work, although there are fewer and fewer places that allow that. Perhaps they're our greatest ally. Whatever, there will be hundreds of occasions when juggling is simply out of the question. Can you see it, in a board meeting? "Cigarette, Peter?" "No, thanks, I'll just play with my balls." Crazy.'

Beth laughed, both at the deliberate double meaning

and at Gideon's vivid imagery. 'No, I can see your point. They could squash one of these quite legitimately, though.'

She threw a stress-ball up into the air and he caught it, his large fist curling round it and snatching it out of the air under her nose just as she went for it. He ended up with her hand trapped inside his against his chest, and for a breathless second they stood locked together. She could feel the warmth of his chest on her hand, and beneath his ribs the solid thud of his heart. She flicked her eyes up to his and surprised a look of yearning in them before the weary shutters came down and he released her, turning away.

'They should be here in a second,' he murmured, and as if he had conjured them the first of their smokers trooped in. The tension dissolved like mist in the morning sunshine, until she was left wondering if it had really been there or if she had simply imagined it.

As Gideon had predicted, they had already lost one of their ten candidates. She had never really been that committed to giving up, apparently, and Gideon had told Beth he had been surprised when she had attended in the first place.

Once all the others were there, the diaries were produced and discussed, and a pattern seemed to emerge. The hardest cigarettes to give up, it was decided, were the first one of the day, the ones after meals, and any in a social context such as the pub. Others, it was thought, would be easier, and so it was decided by the group that those would be the first to go, stretching the time interval between them so that there would be fewer between meals and outside the pub.

'It's a case of having little tricks up your sleeve,' Gideon told them. 'The craving will probably only last three to four minutes each time, so if you can do something—anything!—to occupy your hands in that time, you'll find it easier. Anyone got any suggestions?'

David Hendry chuckled. 'Take the wife to bed?'

His comment was greeted with laughter, but as one man pointed out, that wouldn't help him at all.

'"Confucius say, the three best things in life are a drink before and a fag after",' he told them with a grin, 'and I have to say I agree! That'll be my hardest one to drop.'

'In which case I suggest you find another diversionary tactic,' Gideon said with a chuckle.

Beth then showed them how to do breathing and relaxation exercises to alleviate stress, and Gideon passed round the stress-balls and chewing-gum, and told them the pitfalls of nicotine gum and the relative benefits of patches.

'I would strongly recommend, however, that you try and give up without, because they can become just as addictive as the cigarettes in their way, and remember, you're aiming for control, not just a different master.'

They discussed the dates they would give up, and came to the conclusion that the first of October, that Friday, would be the best day for most of them. Paul Stone, the man Gideon had advised to find a different diversionary tactic, said his daughter was getting married on the second and so he would defer his big day until the Sunday. He felt the stress of the day would defeat any attempt to give up, and Gideon agreed.

Before they left, they all had a go on the 'smoker-

NOTHING LEFT TO GIVE

lyser', a machine for measuring the level of carbon monoxide in the blood.

'You'll be surprised how rapidly that level falls once you're not smoking any more,' Gideon told them.

'If we make it,' Paul said with half-hearted humour.

'You'll make it — think positive and get an ally, someone you can talk to, someone who'll help you get through those few minutes.'

They watched them go, and Beth gathered all the leaflets and aids together and put them back in the cupboard in the corner.

As she finished Gideon appeared at her side, medical bag in hand.

'All done?'

She nodded. 'I'll just get my coat.'

They left together, Gideon flicking off the lights and setting the alarm, and they walked back to the house in the gathering gloom in a companionable silence.

'They seem quite keen,' she said as they rounded the corner by the church.

'Hmm. Hopefully they'll stay that way. What's for supper? I'm starving.'

'You're always starving. It's fish pie and broccoli — you'll find it in the oven, and there's apple flan in the fridge.'

He cranked an eyebrow. 'Aren't you joining me?'

'I ate with the children,' she told him, forcing herself to meet his eye.

For a second she thought he was going to ask her to join him anyway, but then he nodded and turned away.

'Fine. Thank you. I'll see you tomorrow.'

And he scrunched off across the gravel, leaving her alone by the door of the coach house.

She let herself in, made a drink and tried to concentrate on the television.

Fruitless task. She might as well have been watching it in Japanese for all the attention she paid.

All she could think was, if she hadn't eaten with the children, she could now have been sitting with him over a cup of coffee or a glass of wine instead of being up here on her own.

But she hadn't, and there was no way he was going to invite her over now, so she might as well stop fretting about it.

It was a long evening.

She had just finished her surgery on Wednesday morning and was heading out into the square to buy a few things before the shops closed for lunch when she noticed a man coming towards her, clutching a blood-soaked towel to his head.

Two things struck her immediately—one, he was heading for the surgery, and two, he was blind. He was being guided by a blood-smeared Labrador, and she wondered what on earth could have happened to them.

She walked up to him.

'Can I help you? I'm one of the practice nurses.'

'Oh, would you? I've obviously hacked a hole in my head, but I think it will be all right if it's cleaned up and has a dressing on it. Would you be kind enough to have a look?'

'Of course.'

She linked her arm through his and headed back to the surgery, guiding him through the door.

He followed her into her room and instructed the dog to sit, which she did, instantly.

'What happened?' Beth asked him.

'Oh, stupid really. I fell over Katie — I should have known better, she always lies across the doorway, but the doorbell rang and I just stood up and went, and zap — straight over her. I must have caught my head on the corner of the piano.'

Beth eased the soaked towel away from his head and winced.

'Ouch. It's a nasty cut. Let me clean it up to make sure, but I'm afraid it'll need stitches.'

'Damn. Does that mean I'll have to go to the hospital casualty department?'

'Oh, no.' Beth swabbed and tutted. 'Dr Pendragon should be able to do it — he's the duty doctor today. Are you registered with us?'

He nodded. 'Yes, I'm his patient. I play chess with him.'

Beth was surprised. 'How do you remember all the moves?' she asked.

He laughed. 'I have a special pocket set that I use to keep track of it, but in practice I just remember where the pieces are. Sort of mental gymnastics.'

Beth, who couldn't play chess with her eyes open, thought it sounded horribly athletic and said so, just before going out to find Gideon.

'Patient of yours — blind man that you play chess with?'

'Oh, yes, Michael Roberts. What about him?'

'He's just fallen over his dog and cut his forehead open — looks quite nasty. Could you have a look? I think it needs suturing.'

'Daft bugger,' Gideon said affectionately, inspecting the cut. 'That's nasty. You'll need quite a few stitches in it, and the sooner the better. Mind staying on a little, Beth?'

'No, of course not.'

She prepared a suture trolley while Gideon washed his hands and gowned up, and then listened as he chatted to Michael while he infiltrated the area with lignocaine and waited for it to go numb.

It was quite a deep cut, and Gideon brought it together with great care — far more so than many surgeons would be capable of, she thought, and then allowed that she might just be biased.

Finally the suturing was finished and she was able to clear up and leave. By this time the shops had closed and opened again, and she was quizzed by Mabel Robinson who just happened to be in there as well.

'What's young Michael done to himself then?' she asked.

'Fell over the dog. He'll be fine.'

'Poor boy — I remember him as a lad, before he went blind. Lovely boy he was — great future ahead of him. Going to be a vet, but bang — one day he just couldn't see properly, and they found he had a tumour pressing on the nerves. They operated and saved his life, but he's been blind ever since and always will be — took the nerve away with the lump, so Winnie said.'

'Winnie?'

'Does for them, dear. Has done for years — which reminds me, how are you getting on?'

Beth smiled at the less-than-subtle question. 'Fine thanks. In fact, if you'll excuse me, I must buy some ham for the children's packed lunches and then get back to start the supper.'

'You carry on, dear, don't mind me,' Mrs Robinson

said with a smile, and turned to the lady who had just come in behind her.

'Winnie, you'll never guess what — young Michael's fallen over the dog and cut his head open. . .'

Paul Stone's daughter got married on Saturday morning, and Beth watched all the guests arriving at the church from the window of her flat.

It was a lovely day, a bit blowy but clear and bright for a change, and as they all drove away after the wedding Beth spared a thought for Paul and his speech. Oh, well, as soon as it was over he could give up smoking. No doubt the money he saved would come in handy to pay for the wedding — if he wasn't so worried about the cost that he couldn't give up!

A little after six there was a tap on the door, and she opened it to find Gideon there, casually dressed in cords and a jumper.

'Come in,' she said, and stepped back, allowing him in to the hall.

He seemed a little awkward. 'Um — I won't keep you, but Paul Stone asked if we'd like to go down to the pub and have a drink to his daughter later. I wondered if you'd like to come.'

'Oh — well, yes, that would be lovely. What should I wear?'

He shrugged. 'There'll be people there in all sorts, I expect — I should wear what you're comfortable in. I'm going like this.'

'Right. What time?'

'Sevenish?'

'OK. Shall I come over when I'm ready?'

'Fine. See you later.'

He turned on his heel and the door clicked shut behind him just before her muffled shriek of delight.

A date! My God, he really had asked her out for a date! OK, it wasn't a formal dinner or anything, but even so!

Oh, no, clothes!

She sprinted upstairs and ransacked her wardrobe.

Nothing. Absolutely nothing that wasn't too much or too little.

In the end she settled for a pair of leggings and a long, mohair tunic over them, with court shoes to dress it up.

It made her look leggy and elegant, and she was quite happy with the effect.

She scooped her hair back into a ponytail, put on a touch of eyeshadow, mascara and lipstick, and stood back to examine her handiwork.

Fine.

Unfortunately Gideon didn't think so.

'What's wrong?' she asked him as he eyed her thoughtfully.

In answer he reached behind her and pulled out her ponytail band, fanning her hair over her shoulders.

'Better,' he said gruffly. 'Ready?'

She raised an eyebrow. 'Yes — if you're sure I'll pass muster?'

He met her eyes and sighed. 'I'm sorry, was that a little heavy-handed? Humour me, just this once, eh? You've got such beautiful hair, and I hate to see it all tied up like that when it could be free. . .'

He threaded his fingers through it and held them up, letting it filter through them and fall around her shoulders.

'Just like a waterfall — golden rain.'

'You make me sound like a firework,' she said, a trifle breathlessly.

His eyes locked with hers and he smiled crookedly. 'Perhaps you are,' he murmured, and then opened the door. 'Shall we?'

It was crowded in the pub, and very lively. Clearly everyone knew everyone else, and Beth seemed to be the only stranger.

However she soon felt at home. Michael Roberts was there, sitting with a group in the corner with Katie at his feet, the dressing on his head stark white in the murky lighting.

David Hendry was there, too, throwing himself into the spirit of the evening but not, to Beth's surprise, with a cigarette in hand.

There was dancing in the function room, and after they had been there a while David came up to her.

'I've got an urge,' he told her laughingly. 'Come and take my mind off it for four minutes.'

She went, happy to help, happy to belong to this cheerful, jolly crowd.

They danced one dance, but he confessed to still having an urge and claimed her for the next as well.

As it drew to a close Gideon drifted out of the crowd he was with and came over to her, stealing her from David.

'I've got an urge too,' he told her seriously. 'You've got to help me.'

There was a wicked twinkle in his eye, but something else, something that could have been loneliness.

The song started, slow and mellow, and she went into his arms without a word.

He made no attempt to keep a safe distance between

them, and so she laid her head on his chest, the wool of his jumper rough against her cheek, his heart strong and solid under her ear, and let her arms creep round his waist and lie against the strong column of his spine.

As they moved she could feel his thighs brush hers, and his hands slid down to her hips and eased her closer.

The proof of his reaction to her was shocking and yet thrilling at the same time. She stiffened, and then relaxed again, leaning into him and letting the music take them. So what if he wanted her? He wasn't alone, it was quite reciprocal. She was just better able to disguise it.

As the dance finished, his arms dropped and he stepped back.

'Thank you,' he murmured, and she could see something burning in his eyes.

If only she could be sure it was her he burned for, and not just a convenient woman so many years after his wife's death. 'I think I'll go home now,' she told him, suddenly unable to stay there and be social any more.

'I'll come with you. We've done our thing. Come and say goodbye to Paul and his wife.'

They bade their farewells and went out into the darkness of the night. The fine weather of the afternoon had broken, and drizzle misted the air.

They turned up their collars and walked briskly back to the coach house. She wouldn't ask him in, she decided. It was too dangerous.

She turned to him at the door. 'Coffee?' she said before she could stop herself.

'Thanks.'

She unlocked the door and led him inside, shaking out her coat and hanging it in the hall before running up to put the kettle on. With every step she was conscious of him behind her, his large body dwarfing the room, closing in the walls and bringing down the ceiling.

Odd, the bed seemed to grow too. She fiddled at the sink, and he squatted down in front of her stereo system and flicked through her CDs.

'Mind if I put something on?' he asked.

'No — try the Clannad.'

'I was going to.'

They exchanged surprised, tentative smiles. While she made the coffee he put the CD on and made himself at home on the sofa, leaving her the option of sitting on it too and being much too close to him, or sitting on the bed and appearing provocative.

In the end she handed him his coffee and sat on the floor leaning against the end of the bed.

They drank their coffee in companionable silence interspersed with the odd comment about the wedding party, and then finally there was nothing left to do but look at each other.

'Come here,' he said softly, and after an endless moment she stood up and moved over to the sofa, curling up in the opposite corner.

He reached a long arm along the back and wrapped it round her shoulders, drawing her closer.

Then his head came down and his eyes drifted shut just as his lips brushed hers.

He tasted of whisky and coffee and something else, something personal and his alone. Her arms slid round his shoulders and linked behind his head, her fingers threading through the soft, thick mass of his black hair, and he groaned deep in his throat.

'Open your mouth,' he murmured against her lips,

and she obeyed mindlessly, relishing the invasion of his tongue as it sought the secret recesses of her mouth and stroked them into flames.

One hand threaded through her hair, the other went to her thigh and slid beneath the tunic, sliding up under it and cupping one breast in warm, firm fingers.

'So soft,' he whispered, and his mouth left hers and nipped and nibbled down over her cheek, down to the hollow of her throat, then round behind her ear, his tongue making little forays into the sensitive shell.

She gasped and he laughed, a low, throaty laugh of masculine satisfaction.

'Oh, Beth,' he said softly, and rested his forehead against hers. 'So lovely, so sweet and innocent. I must go.'

She knew he was right, but the sharp ache of loss nearly made her cry out.

'Yes, I suppose you must,' she said after a moment, and was surprised at how steady her voice sounded.

He stood up and kissed her lightly on the forehead, pressing her back into the seat when she would have stood up.

'I'll see myself out — you stay there.'

She closed her eyes and dropped her head back, listening to the ringing of his shoes on the spiral staircase and his softly murmured, 'Goodnight,' just as the door clicked shut.

Then she was alone with her thoughts, and they kept her awake most of the night.

When she did sleep, it was to dream of him again, of the big bed and Gideon's strong arms around her, his lips on hers, his heart beating against her own.

*   *   *

He was a fool. Why had he done that? It had been bad enough before he'd tasted her. Now it would be impossible.

He didn't even bother to go to bed. Instead he poured himself a scotch and went into his study. In the rack by the CD player was a Clannad album, the same one he had put on in Beth's flat.

He put it on again, torturing himself, and slouched in the leather settee with the drink and let his mind run riot.

CHAPTER FOUR

BETH had a feeling that Gideon was avoiding her after that night.

She wasn't sure, though, because *she* was so busy avoiding *him* it was hard to tell, but she just had a feeling. . .

Not that avoiding him was doing her any good. He still occupied most of her waking thoughts, and as for her dreams — well, they were almost unprintable!

She had started eating with the children at the slightest excuse, and at least three nights of the week she would be able to avoid seeing him altogether except for a very brief hand-over as he arrived and she left.

And she made sure she was never in his bedroom again when he got home, and she forced herself to think about something quite different when she folded the washing and ironed his shirts.

Then one morning she was unable to avoid him. It was seven-thirty, and she heard a knock on her door.

'Beth? It's Gideon. Can I have a word?'

She was half dressed, so she quickly flung on her dressing-gown and ran down to the door.

He was wearing his running gear, his hair rumpled, and sweat beaded his top lip. He looked incredibly masculine and very, very desirable.

She tugged the gown closer. 'What's the matter?' she asked.

'Claire. She won't come out of her room, and she says

she wants to see you. She won't let me in, and she sounds upset.'

Beth stared at him. 'Any ideas?'

He shook his head. 'Unless—her periods haven't started yet.'

'Ah. OK. Give me a minute to get dressed and I'll come over.'

She shut the door and ran back upstairs, pulled on her dress, scraped her hair up into a bun and slapped on a touch of lipstick. Then she went into the bathroom for the necessary, just in case, and, grabbing her bag, she ran back downstairs and over to the house.

'She's still in there,' Gideon informed her. He was making sandwiches, a towel slung round his neck, and she went past him and tapped on Claire's bedroom door.

'Claire? It's Beth.'

The lock turned with a click, and after a second Beth pushed the door open. Claire was standing in the room, still in her dressing-gown, and looking utterly miserable and desperately embarrassed.

'You wanted to see me?'

She nodded.

'What's up, lovey?' Beth asked her gently.

Her eyes welled and the blush deepened. 'I wish my Mum was here,' she said unsteadily.

'Period?' Beth offered, and the unhappy girl nodded.

'My sheets are devastated, and Dad'll go crazy—oh, God, it's just so *humiliating*!'

Beth gave her a hug. 'Don't worry, sweetheart, it happens to us all, and your father won't go in the least crazy. Have you got any sanitary towels?'

She nodded. 'Dad got me some ages ago.'

'Right—go and sort yourself out and get ready for school. I'll do your bed.'

She hesitated at the door. 'Will you tell Dad?'

'He's guessed.'

'Oh.' She fiddled with her dressing-gown belt for a minute. 'What about William?'

'What about him? It's none of his business—unless you want to tell him?'

'Maybe later,' she muttered and went out, and Beth went back down to the kitchen. Gideon was finishing off the lunches and Will was nowhere to be seen.

He hitched an eyebrow in her direction.

'She's OK. She's just getting ready.'

'Was I right?'

She nodded. 'She's OK now. It's just a bit of a shock the first time.'

'She could always have the day off.'

'What, and arouse even more comment? I don't think so. She'll be fine.'

Gideon sighed. 'Thank God you were here. I try and be mother and father to them, but there are just times when girls need a woman——' He broke off and hugged her. 'Thank you, Beth.'

She slid her arms round him, sweaty running-shirt and all, and hugged him back. Oh, it felt so good to hold him again. . .

He released her and turned towards the door. 'Come on, William, you'll miss the bus. Here's your lunch. What are you having for breakfast?'

Will eyed them curiously. 'What's Beth doing here?'

'She's come for breakfast. Am I doing you toast or what?'

'Yeah—have you seen my rugby kit?'

'It's in your sports bag in the utility room,' Beth told him. 'Will, have you seen Sophie?'

Just then the two girls came into the room, Sophie in a snuggly jumper and leggings, Claire in her uniform looking proud and very vulnerable all at once.

Gideon shot her a grin, winked and passed her a piece of toast. 'Eat — you're going to be late. Do you want Ready-Brek, Tuppence?'

'Toast.'

'Oh.' Gideon handed her his piece of toast, and glanced at his watch. 'Oh, hell — Beth, you couldn't stay with Sophie while I shower, could you? Make sure she has something to eat and drink, and I'll be down in ten minutes.'

Claire and William ran out a couple of minutes later, leaving Beth with the little one.

'Your hair's a mess, sweetheart — would you like me to put it in a ponytail for you?'

She nodded, her mouth too busy with the toast to speak, and while she ate Beth brushed the pretty golden curls and drew them up into a high ponytail.

'There — gorgeous!'

She kissed the jammy little mouth and Sophie grinned at her, slipping off the stool to go and find something in the cupboard to take for break time.

Finally, just when Beth thought she was going to have to take her to school, Gideon ran down the stairs and quickly bundled her into her coat.

'You're a treasure, Beth,' he said fervently, and pressed a quick kiss on her lips. 'Ugh, jam.'

She smiled. 'Sophie's.'

He grinned and winked. 'See you later.'

As she closed the door behind them, the fantasy came back with a vengeance.

Oh, well, since she was here playing mother, she might as well clear the breakfast table and empty the dishwasher. . .

From that moment on, she and Claire were firm friends. The girl seemed to grow up overnight, becoming helpful, co-operative and actively seeking out Beth's company.

Beth had been surprised to find what good company she was, and they had often worked together after Claire got back from school, the girl doing her homework on the kitchen table while Sophie helped her with the supper. Now, though, there was another dimension, as if they were in the same league somehow, and Beth felt curiously protective towards the fledgling woman.

And, strangely, the new closeness between her and Claire seemed to ease the tension between her and Gideon. He began to relax more around her, so she could see even more clearly how wonderful it would be to be his wife.

In fact, she thought, it probably wouldn't be so very different. She was already doing most of the things a wife would do. It was only those parts of a marriage that haunted her dreams that were missing, and Beth began to wonder if she shouldn't take the leap and encourage Gideon in that direction.

However he hadn't kissed her again, not since the night of Paul's daughter's wedding — except for the brief peck on the morning of Claire's entry to womanhood, and she wondered if he had only kissed her that night because she was there.

It was Monday again, and after fetching Sophie from school and cooking a meal she ran back to the coach house in the rain, changed into her uniform again and drove to the surgery for the smoking cessation clinic.

It was a filthy night, and she was wondering if any of the patients would use it as an excuse not to come. It was their fourth meeting, nearly four weeks since she had arrived, and things were hotting up for them.

They were now all non-smokers, except for the odd failure every now and then, and as Gideon was at pains to point out, everyone was allowed the odd mistake — just so long as it didn't become a habit!

David Hendry was doing very well, having given up as he had said he would on the first of October and not touched another cigarette since.

Only one other patient, a pregnant woman called Jan Driscoll, had also succeeded one hundred per cent.

Paul, on the other hand, had failed repeatedly, and always with the same cigarette, the first one in the morning.

'Try jogging,' Gideon advised, and was jeered by the men.

'All right for you, mate,' Paul grumbled cheerfully, 'you can get up at a civilised hour. I have to be up at five for the milking, then out again straight after breakfast, round the farm. When do you suggest I jog?'

Gideon grinned. 'When you find time to smoke.'

'What, after I turn out the last cow and go back in for my breakfast? While Jill cooks it, I have a cup of tea and a cigarette — what am I supposed to do, jog round the table?'

They all laughed. 'Have cereal, so you don't have to hang around waiting,' Jan suggested.

He looked doubtful, but said he'd try. 'Got to succeed — have to pay for the damn wedding, don't I?' he laughed.

Beth then talked about diet, and asked how many of them found they were eating compulsively. It was the women, stuck at home all day, who found the eating part the hardest.

'Find something else to do — turning out the kitchen cupboards, or knitting, for instance.'

David Hendry agreed. 'My wife's doing a crochet blanket for one of these relief agencies, using up all her old scraps of wool — she taught me how and I do a bit every time I get that urge.'

Paul laughed. 'Oh, yeah, I can just see me up in the cab of a tractor with my knitting!'

They all laughed with him, and after a few minutes when Beth advised them on healthier eating and gave them booklets on eating for a healthy heart, they all headed for the door.

When David opened it, a gust of wind snatched it from his hand and rain sprayed in all over them.

'Good lord, it's coming down like stair-rods!' Paul said worriedly, peering out into the night. 'I'd better get off and move those cows up to the barn. River's damn near the top as it is after the weekend.'

Others murmured agreement, and Beth quickly cleared up and pulled on her coat.

'I don't suppose you've got your car here, have you?' Gideon asked her.

'I have, it was raining when I came back.'

'Thank God for that. Right, shall we go?'

Beth ran over to the car while Gideon locked up, and

he folded himself into the seat and ran his hands through his streaming hair.

'It's coming down in torrents! If it keeps this up we'll be in trouble.'

'Does the river really flood?'

'Oh, yes — when it's wet enough. It's only done it once in the fifteen years I've been here, but it's pretty dramatic. There are several houses that flood, and all the roads are affected.'

Beth started the car and drove slowly home, her windscreen wipers barely keeping pace with the torrential rain that lashed the car.

'Good job it's not far,' she muttered.

'Go past the lane and on a bit — I'd like to see the river,' he told her.

She crossed the square and followed the road out the other side, and after a few yards they reached a little bridge.

'Hang on,' he yelled, and jumping out of the car, he ran to the bridge. A few seconds later he ran back and slammed the door behind him. 'It's within a foot of the top — I reckon it'll go over, even if the rain stops now. It's all the water coming off the fields that'll do the damage.'

She turned round and as she headed back, a police car passed her.

'That's Philip Horn, the local bobby. He'll be checking on the water level. If he thinks it's bad enough they'll open the church hall and put people up there for the night.'

'They'll be soaked and frozen,' Beth said worriedly.

'And shocked. I'll go over there, I think. Let's get back and I'll check the children are all right, then I'll go on down. They might want to use the Discovery to help get people out.'

Beth pulled up outside the coach house. 'Can I come too? Give you a hand?'

He hesitated. 'Do you want to?'

'Yes—yes, of course. People could well be hurt climbing out of windows and trying to rescue their possessions. Should we collect some supplies from the surgery?'

'Good idea. Look, you go on in and change—have you got wellies and a good coat?'

'Wellies, yes, but only this mac that's even slightly waterproof.'

'I'll bring you William's old waxed jacket—it's got a hood, and it'll keep most of the weather out. I'll see you in a tick.'

He headed for the house at a run, and Beth took a deep breath and dashed over to the coach house just feet away. By the time she had fiddled with the key she was soaked to the skin, the mac no protection at all against the vile weather.

She hung it up, ran up and changed into warm leggings, a shirt and a warm jumper, and pulled on some thick socks to wear under her wellies.

By the time Gideon returned with William's coat she was ready, her hair scraped back into a ponytail and tucked down her neck, wellies on.

'Good girl,' he said approvingly, and handed her the jacket. 'I mucked out the pockets—crisp packets and God knows what. Evil child.'

She chuckled. 'Have you spoken to anyone on the phone?'

'Police—they said it's bad further south and the

forecast is for more of the same for the next few hours at least.'

Beth stared at him. 'But the river's nearly at the top——'

'It's over. We need to move.'

He told her to stay there while he got the Discovery out of the garage, and then he asked for her keys and put her car away out of the rain.

She was waiting for him in the passenger seat when he climbed back up, hair dripping.

'Right, surgery for emergency medical supplies and blankets, then down to the church hall.'

When they arrived there were already a few people there—the vicar, dressed in wellingtons and a voluminous waterproof, his wife in the kitchen getting the kettle on, and the policeman, Philip Horn, organising relief supplies and delegating to the men who had turned up to help.

One by one the people came, their faces telling it all. Some, the older ones who had lost everything before, were silent with resignation, others wept and railed against fate. Children cried, confused and frightened by the force of the water, and Beth's heart went out to them.

They looked like the pictures of refugees on television, she thought sadly.

Many of them had minor cuts and bruises, and Beth dressed their wounds and tried to cheer them up.

The men had left to go about their tasks, sandbagging doorways and rescuing those trapped by the steadily rising floodwaters.

One woman's hand was crushed where she had been holding the door knob and opened the door to escape, only to have it flung back against the wall by the force of the water.

Beth immobilised it, and then Judith Wight, one of Gideon's partners, arrived to see if she could help.

'Judith, you couldn't have a look at this, could you?'

'Sure — oh, nasty. I think that looks like a fracture, Mrs Griggs. Tell you what, we'll just leave it like that splinted for now, and I'll give you an injection for the pain and we'll get you to hospital to have it properly looked at as soon as the water goes down.'

Beth made her as comfortable as possible, and settled her in the corner with a drink in her other hand.

Another of the evacuees, a man called Brian Hurley, had a huge sliver of wood driven into the ball of his thumb. It was clearly extremely painful, and Beth helped Judith set up a small sterile area and remove the splinter. Judith had to open the skin to get a purchase on the wood, and because of the profuse bleeding it was difficult to see if all the little splinters had come away. Having infiltrated it with local anaesthetic it was easy to examine, but consequently there was no feedback from the patient to help establish if there was any residue.

In the end Judith stitched the ragged entry hole with a single suture and asked him to come to the surgery in the morning for a clean dressing and a check.

As the evening wore on, Mabel Robinson appeared at Beth's elbow, bedraggled but safe.

'I didn't realise your house flooded,' Beth said to her in surprise.

'Oh, no, dear, I've just come to make sure all my friends are all right and give a hand, really — not that I'm much use these days, but I can sit and talk to people, take their mind off it, eh?'

Beth was amazed by the community spirit. Everybody pulled together, working like Trojans to lift furniture out of the way of the flood waters, gathering up treasured possessions and putting them in bedrooms above the reach of the waer.

The rescue workers popped in every now and again to get drinks and give them an update on the situation, and they themselves were frozen and exhausted.

Gideon came in at one stage for a cup of tea, and told her that although it had stopped raining the flood waters had reached four feet in part of the town.

Beth was staggered. Four feet — that was half way to the ceiling, all the way to Mabel Robinson's chin almost. Certainly over little Sophie's head.

She looked round again at the children, seeing the flood now from their little eyes, and her sympathy increased a hundredfold.

She went into the kitchen to see if she could make them a hot drink of cocoa or something, and while she was working she overheard Mabel Robinson and a couple of the friends on the other side of the hatch in the main part of the hall.

' — such a lovely man, Dr Pendragon. He works so hard, and never thinks of himself.'

'Those children have never wanted for anything ——'

'Except a good mother. They've needed that for a long while!'

'Oh, don't. That woman was no good — no good at all. I remember before Claire was born — still, that's all water under the bridge. And him bringing up that little cuckoo as if she's his ——'

'What about that nurse, then, the new one? They seem pretty thick.'

'Beth?' Mrs Robinson said. 'She'd be good for him. Lovely girl, that. Just what the whole lot of them needs, but I fancy he's too busy to even notice her. Anyway, I expect she thinks he's too old for her.'

'Oh, I don't know — plenty of life left in him yet. And didn't you say she blushed when you asked about the flat?'

Beth had heard enough. She made the cocoa and carried it out of the kitchen and over to the children, praying that her blush would have faded by the time Mrs Robinson and her friends noticed her. The mothers took the cocoa from her gratefully, and after a while the children settled down in their makeshift beds and began to fall asleep.

Shortly after midnight the lights flickered and went out, and there was a short spell of darkness lit only by the emergency exit lights while the pub landlord went back for some candles.

The darkness was absolute, and Beth could feel the panic rising, but then the vicar's wife started singing campfire songs.

Someone else produced a storm lantern, and in a short while the tension eased a little, warmed by the singing and by the atmosphere of caring and support.

Gideon came back again then, and drew her outside.

'I'm worried about Michael,' he told her. 'I haven't seen him, and although his cottage isn't usually flooded, it is fairly low and if the river water got high enough, it could reach his garden and run down to the cottage. If that happens, he could be in serious trouble.'

'Is it likely?'

He shrugged. 'I don't know. I was going to take the Discovery and go and have a look — want to come?'

She nodded. 'Yes, yes I will. Let me get my coat.'

She joined him a moment later, with not only her coat but also a few supplies from the surgery — dressing packs, a splint, a blanket, even a lightweight stretcher.

'Good thinking,' Gideon said approvingly, and Beth felt a foolish rush of pride. Absurd, really, when she was only doing her job.

She climbed up into the Discovery and they set off, taking a roundabout route to avoid the flooded lanes.

'I'll have to go over this field and we may get stuck — then again, we may not,' Gideon told her with a laugh. He changed down to the low ratio gearbox and the car chewed smoothly through the muddy gateway and across the rough stubble of the field towards Michael's cottage.

As they approached, Beth could see water in the headlights.

Gideon swore softly. 'It's worse than I'd thought. I'll take the car as close as I dare, but then I think we'll have to do the rest on foot.'

'Can't you get on to the lane? It looks as if it's above the water level.'

Gideon peered into the darkness, and shrugged. 'We'll give it a whirl — certainly make it easier.'

He drove through into the next field and out on to Michael's lane, then headed back towards the Square. In fact he was able to park right outside the cottage, but as they climbed out Beth could see the cause of the problem.

Although the water hadn't reached the lane at that point, the cottage and its garden were set below the level of the road, and in the light of Gideon's torch she could see water swirling round the cottage. It was almost up to the window sills, and as they approached she wondered how on earth they would get him out.

'The front door's open. I expect he opened it to come out and couldn't shut it again. He may be safe, of course. His family live about half a mile away — they may well have come over and picked him up. I'll call.'

Gideon leant over the gate, cupped his hands round his mouth and yelled, 'Michael? Are you there?'

They strained their ears, but all they could hear was the rushing and gurgling of water.

'I'll have to go in — you stay here, and if necessary take the car and go and get help.'

He was just about to go down the steps towards the cottage when Katie, Michael's labrador, came bounding down the lane.

'Hello, girl,' Gideon said worriedly. 'Where is he, then? Where's Michael?'

She barked and headed down the steps, out into the water. She was a strong swimmer but Beth could see her being carried along by the current. Eventually she reached the open door and struggled in.

She barked again, and Gideon looked back at Beth. 'I think he's in there. Perhaps he let her out to get help. I'm going in.'

'Be careful — the current's strong.'

He nodded, then, stripping off his coat and jumper, he plunged into the water. She heard a gasp, and a muttered comment about brass monkeys, and then he was struggling across the gap towards the door.

As he reached it, Katie appeared in the opening, whining and barking.

'All right, sweetheart, I'm coming,' he soothed, and then seizing the doorpost, he pulled himself into the cottage, leaving Beth standing on the lane in the dark shivering.

After an age he appeared in an upstairs window. 'I've found him — he's hurt, but he's alive. I think he must have tried to get out and got trapped by the water — Katie must have dragged him up the stairs. I'll bring him out but we'll need a stretcher and someone to help. Can you get a rope from the back of the car, tie it to the front bumper and throw the other end to me? I'll make a handrail — just to be on the safe side — I'd hate to drown him.'

She did as she was told, her fingers shaking with the cold, then threw the free end across towards the open front door. He caught it on her third attempt, and tied it to the door chain.

'Right, can you go back to the village and get help?'

Beth thought quickly. She had the collapsible stretcher in the car, and if she braved the water they could probably get him out more quickly — and as he was unconscious, time was of the essence.

'Hang on, I'm coming.'

'Beth, no!'

'Yes — there isn't time to do anything else!'

Ignoring his protests, she ran to the car, retrieved the stretcher and ran back to the steps. It was easier for her than it had been for Gideon because of the rope handrail, but still the cold and the sheer force of the water caught her by surprise.

By the time she reached the safety of the doorway, she was badly frightened and exhausted, but there was no time to worry about herself.

Following Gideon she made her way across the room and saw in the light of Gideon's torch that Michael was sprawled halfway up the stairs, the water up to his thighs. Together they fitted the stretcher together and lifted Michael on to it.

'I don't think he's got any spinal injuries, but keep him as flat as possible,' Gideon instructed as they moved him from his awkward position on the stairs.

As they turned to go towards the front door, Beth heard a splash and they were plunged into darkness.

Gideon swore fluently.

'I take it you dropped the torch?' Beth said drily.

'Ha bloody ha. Are you ready?'

'Yes.'

'Right.'

It was harder than coming in, far harder, what with the stretcher and the pitch darkness to contend with, but after an age they managed to struggle back to the steps and up to the lane.

Beth had opened the back of the Discovery and folded the rear seats down, and they laid Michael in the back.

'He needs medical attention fast — let's take him back to the surgery and get him warm and dry and find out what's wrong.'

Katie jumped in beside Michael, and Beth climbed into the back and supported his head while Gideon reversed up the lane, drove back over the field and then round to the surgery.

Once there they carried Michael into Gideon's office and switched on a fan heater, and together they stripped the unconscious man and wrapped him in lightweight cellular blankets while Katie sat by his head, whining softly and licking him. He had a huge, ugly purpling bruise on his temple, close to the recent injury from his previous fall. This one, however, had obviously been more serious although the skin wasn't broken.

'What about the dog licking him?' Beth asked.

Gideon glanced at Katie and shrugged. 'It's more likely to do him good than harm. I should let her get on with it.' He checked Michael over for fractures and other injuries he might have missed in his initial examination, which as he pointed out had hardly been in ideal circumstances. There were few, and those that there were seemed to be superficial.

'So why is he still unconscious?'

'Hypothermia? What's his temperature?'

'Thirty-five in his mouth, but I'd rather take it rectally. Can we roll him over?'

'Sure.' Gideon helped her roll him to his side, and she inserted the thermometer and waited thirty seconds.

'Nearly thirty-six.'

'That's better. OK, well, I think he ought to go to hospital as fast as possible, and have this head injury investigated——'

Just then Michael groaned, and Katie's tongue shot out and swiped his face. 'Katie?' he croaked, and she whined and lashed her tail.

Gideon picked up his hand and squeezed it reassuringly. 'Michael, it's all right. You're at the surgery. Michael, can you hear me?'

His sightless eyes flickered open, and he turned his head. 'Gideon?'

'Yes. It's all right, you're safe. We got you out.'

'Out?' His brow furrowed, and then recollection came. 'Oh, God, the water—my computer——'

'Bugger your computer, you nearly died. What happened?'

He swallowed. 'Water everywhere — I opened the door — it must have surged in and knocked me over.' He lifted a hand to his head and fingered the bump gingerly. 'Ouch. Have I been out long?'

'I don't know — what time did you open the door?'

'Oh — eleven-thirty?'

Gideon glanced at his watch. 'Nearly two hours.'

'I haven't been out all the time — I seem to remember waking up on the stairs, about God knows how I got there.'

Gideon glanced at the dog. 'I think Katie might have had something to do with it. She was out when we arrived, and came running back and led me in. She must have gone for help.'

'Good girl, Katie — well done,' he said shakily, and his eyes filled with tears. 'Oh, God, I was scared — I could feel the water swirling round my legs when I was on the stairs, and I couldn't find the strength to climb up. . .'

Beth laid a reassuring hand on his shoulder and squeezed gently. 'It's OK, Michael. It's all over.'

'Can you feel everything now?' Gideon asked him.

'Yes — everything, every last damn bump! I hurt everywhere.'

'I expect the water surging in swept you into the furniture.'

Michael gave a hollow laugh. 'Certainly feels like it.'

Gideon glanced at Beth. 'You ought to go to hospital for tests, Michael — make sure you're all right after that bump.'

'How do I get there?' he asked bluntly. 'Fly?'

Gideon sighed. He had a point. He was clearly less

badly hurt than they had at first suspected, although with a head injury you could never be too careful.

'How about if I take you back to my place and keep an eye on you tonight, then we get you in tomorrow if I feel it's necessary?'

'Sounds good,' he said tiredly. 'My head aches.'

'I'm sure. Look, see if you can get up for me, can you? You're on the floor at the moment. Here, sit up and put this gown on.'

Carefully, testing his limbs as he went, Michael sat up, struggling into the proffered gown and then got to his feet.

'Oh, God, my head's thrashing.'

Gideon tucked a blanket round him. 'I'm sure. Come on, if you were in a Dick Francis novel it would be all in a day's work.'

Michael snorted. 'Just find me a bed.'

'All gratitude, this man,' Gideon threw at Beth, and she smiled at him.

She knew he didn't really want gratitude. He had done what he had done because he had no choice. He was that sort of person, and nothing and no one would change him. It was a comforting thought.

She followed the pair of them out, Katie at Michael's heels, and they made their way back to the house.

After Michael was settled in bed they went down to the kitchen.

'I suppose I'd better get cleaned up and get to bed,' Beth said reluctantly.

'Mmm. I'll walk you back.'

The rain had stopped long ago, and they could hear the trees sighing.

Beth tipped her head up and peered at the trees. 'The wind's picking up.'

'Yes, they said it would.' Gideon turned her towards him and searched her face with warm, gentle eyes. 'Will you be OK?' he asked her softly.

'Yes — once I've had a hot shower and got cleaned up a bit. How about you?'

His mouth tipped into a smile. 'I'm fine.'

He drew her into his arms and rested his head against hers. 'Thank you for helping me get him out. You were right, we couldn't afford to leave him there. As it happens it wouldn't have mattered, but we didn't know that at the time. It took a lot of courage getting in that water.'

'You should know,' she replied. 'You did it first.'

He laughed and hugged her. 'But I'm bigger than you; it's easier. Go on now, go and get cleaned up and have a sleep, you'll feel better.'

He opened her door and pushed her gently towards it.

Almost stumbling with exhaustion, she made her way up the spiral staircase, showered and dried her hair briefly and fell into bed. She was asleep in seconds.

CHAPTER FIVE

TUESDAY dawned clear and bright, if a little windy. Apart from a few flattened plants there was nothing to show for the havoc of the night before, Beth thought as she looked out of the window.

She was already up and dressed, and went over to the house to find out how Michael was.

'Much better,' Gideon told her. 'I managed to get through to his father last night on their mobile phone, and his parents were vastly reassured. They couldn't get out of their drive to check up on him, but they weren't that worried because the cottage has never flooded before — at least not that they could remember. He's asleep now, but he's been fine. I'll see what the flooding's like before we decide about sending him in to hospital. Fancy a drive down to the village?'

'Sure — have we got time?'

He nodded. 'I'm keeping the children at home today until we see how the situation develops. Claire and Will won't get to school anyway, and if the village school's open Sophie can go down later.'

They went in the Discovery, with plastic bags over the soggy seats to protect their clothes, and as they drove out of the square and down the worst affected lane, they could see the carnage left by the receding waters.

Some gardens were still flooded, but most now were simply sodden and covered in mud.

Beth sniffed. 'There's a bit of a reek,' she commented.

'Hmm. The sewage system had a bit of a battering — I think we might find we have a few cases of gastroenteritis cropping up in the next twenty-four hours. At least the road's passable now, just about.'

They cut round in a circle and came back in on another road, past Paul Stone's farm. He was standing leaning on a gate, staring out over a field, a cigarette clamped firmly between his lips.

Gideon pulled up beside him.

'Problems?'

He snorted. 'You might say that. Two of my best milkers drowned, five others aborted in the night, sixty acres of potatoes under water, my linseed's flattened and sprouting — it's a bloody disaster, boy.'

He drew deeply on the cigarette, glared at it and threw it in a puddle. 'A real bitch.'

'I'm sorry,' Gideon said quietly. 'How's the house?'

'Oh, fine — and the family's all right, so I suppose that's all that maters.'

They left him being philosophical, and drove out towards Michael's cottage. As Gideon had expected, his parents were there and thanked him again profusely. 'We were so grateful when you rang — we'd tried to phone him and the lines were down, but of course with the mobiles it doesn't matter. I wish he'd get one so we could keep in touch.'

Gideon gave them a rueful smile. 'Perhaps he doesn't like to think it's necessary, and you must admit last night was exceptional.'

His father grunted. 'Damn well hope so. Never

happened before in all the time we've been here, so I suppose you might be right.'

'What's the damage like?' Beth asked.

His father rolled his eyes. 'Terrible — thick mud on the floor, and all the furniture and kitchen units and so on downstairs are ruined.'

'His computer?' Gideon said.

'Oh, finished. The floppies are safe, tell him, on the top of the filing cabinet, but damn all else.'

'I'll tell him. Right, must get on.'

Gideon turned the car round and drove back, taking it steady through the muddy water that still covered one section of the road.

'It doesn't look too bad today, does it?' Beth said wonderingly. 'When you think of all that water around his house last night, and now, if it wasn't for the odd bit of water still lying here and there and the mud in the gardens you'd think nothing had happened.'

He dropped Beth off at the surgery and went back to the house to see Michael and arrannge for an ambulance to take him to the nearest hospital for a head X-ray, and Beth went in and spoke to Molly, who was trying to make sense of the plundered stores.

'Just what did you take?'

Beth laughed. 'God only knows — whatever seemed like a good idea at the time. Look, Brian Hurley should be coming in this morning to see one of us. He had a nasty sliver of wood in his hand and Judith took it out. Can you send him in to me?'

'Sure — oh, and Mrs Robinson's here. Her ulcer dressing got wet and nasty last night, and she thinks it ought to be changed.'

'Right — let me have the list.'

She scanned the names, and went out into the waiting room, calling her first patient.

Jenny Sorrell had come for a well-person check, and first Beth asked her all the usual questions about diet, smoking and drinking habits and breast examination.

'Right,' she said with a smile, 'could you just pop your tights and pants off and climb up on the couch so I can do a smear?'

While she did so Beth donned gloves and prepared the trolley.

'You do know how to do it, I suppose?' the woman asked, only half jokingly.

Beth laughed. 'Oh, yes, don't worry, I know what I'm doing and I'm very thorough. Just pop your heels up by your bottom and let your legs relax for me — that's lovely.'

After inserting the speculum and using the spatula to sweep both the inner edge of the cervix and the outer edge, Beth removed the instruments and told the woman she could get dressed again.

While she prepared the sample for the lab, she asked her patient if she had any problems or queries.

'Well — not really. It's just that since I went into the menopause, I've had a bit of a problem with dryness. Normally it doesn't make any difference, but — well, it's affecting our relationship now, because I get sore very easily.'

Beth wrote 'dyspareunia' in the notes, the medical shorthand for painful intercourse, and asked if they had tried using gynaecological jelly.

'Yes — I get sore with that. My friend said I ought to go on HRT, but there's no family history of osteoporosis, and I really don't want to muck about with nature, but — well, frankly we both miss our sex life.'

Beth had an idea. 'There's a product you could try — it's been around for a while and I've heard very good reports. One of the women at my last practice swore by it. It's a vaginal moisturiser, and as well as moisturising it's also been found to improve vaginal health. You use it about three times a week, and you can buy it over the counter. Here.' She wrote the brand name on a piece of paper and handed it to Mrs Sorrell. 'Give it a whirl. If it doesn't work, come back and talk to your GP about the problem. Maybe you'd only need a very low level of HRT to sort you out.'

She waved the piece of paper. 'I'll try this first — thank you ever so much!'

Beth saw her out, and after inoculating a baby against measles, she changed Mrs Robinson's ulcer dressing.

'Oh, it looks rather sore, my dear. Have you been doing too much?'

'Well, tell you the truth I was up a long while last evening.'

Beth smiled. 'You and me both.'

'Heard you got young Michael out in the nick of time.'

'Well, hardly. The water was already going down when we arrived, I think, so I don't suppose he would have come to any great harm, apart from being cold, wet and frightened.'

'Heard he banged his head.'

Good lord, she thought, the tom-toms *have* been at it! 'Yes, he did, but he's fine now.'

'Gone to hospital, though — just to be on the safe side, I expect.'

'That's right,' Beth agreed, as there was little point in denying it. Patient confidentiality only worked when it had a chance, and clearly Mrs Robinson was more up to date than she was!

She finished changing the hydrocolloid dressing, advised Mrs Robinson to go home and rest for a few days, and after seeing her out she called Mr Hurley in.

'Hello, how are you?' she asked brightly.

'Oh, sore, you know. When the anaesthetic wore off — well! Still, it's not too bad, and she made a lovely neat job. I saw that spike sticking out last night and I thought — hospital job for sure. I was surprised when Dr Wight did it on the spot.'

Beth smiled. 'We don't send you in for fun — not unless we have to. Right, let's have a look under this dressing, shall we?'

In fact the wound was looking very sore and angry, and Beth could see that it was infected.

'Oh, dear. I think you'll need some antibiotics for that today — have you got an appointment with a doctor?'

He shook his head. 'Pendragon's my GP. Think he ought to take a look?'

'I do, yes. That wood could well have been carrying a lot of germs.'

'From the sewer, I suppose? Not a very nice thought, is it?'

'No, I'm afraid it isn't, but we have to consider it. Let me give him a ring and see what he says.'

She caught him just between patients, and he tapped on the door seconds later and came in.

'Hello, Mr Hurley. Gather you got spiked.'

'Yes — stupid, really. I was using an old bit of wood out of the garden to try and wedge the rabbit hutch up out of the water, and the darned thing broke and I ended up stuck on the end. Finished putting the boy's rabbit up out of the way first, though, before I came along to the hall.'

'Hmm. Well, you've certainly got an infection in there. Are you all right with penicillin?'

'Yes — take anything, I can.'

'Right. How's your tetanus — up to date?'

He snorted. 'Got me on that last time I was in, Doc.'

'Well, you'd better have a booster, and I'll give you an injection of penicillin and a prescription for more antibiotics. Then I think you'd better go home to bed — if you've got one at the moment?'

He snorted again. 'Not round ours. Bungalow, isn't it? We're up my sister's.'

Gideon nodded. 'Well, you'll have to take it easy and stay away from all that mud. It's laden with germs and the last place your hand needs to be at the moment. Once it's settled you can do something in rubber gloves, but I should get your family to wear them as well anyway, because you can't be too careful.'

Beth redressed the wound while Gideon drew up the antibiotic and tetanus shots. After he had gone, Beth turned to Gideon.

'How's Michael?'

'Gone to hospital.'

Beth chuckled. 'So Mrs Robinson told me.'

'Good grief, she's surpassed herself.'

'Hmm — she's overdone it, too. Her leg looked much worse.'

'Oh, damn. I have a feeling it's going to be thoroughly resistant to treatment, that ulcer.'

'You don't think she keeps it going so she can come in and natter to us, do you?'

Gideon laughed. 'I wouldn't put it past her. Oh, well, keep an eye on her for me, could you? We'll watch it and if it doesn't improve, we'll try something else.'

'Like what — witchcraft?'

Gideon chuckled.

'Something like that.'

It was an odd sort of day. Her antenatal clinic that afternoon was routine enough, except that every conversation with every woman was dominated by the events of the previous night.

One woman failed to attend, and Molly said she'd phoned and complained of a tummy bug.

It was the beginning of a wave of gastroenteritis that swept the part of the village that had been flooded.

All residents were instructed to stop drinking the tap water, and bottled water was shipped in by the water authority and the system checked and flushed through with heavily chlorinated water to kill any residual germs before the supply was reconnected.

Nevertheless the cure was too late for many, and that night Beth heard Gideon coming and going for hours in the Discovery.

He was on call anyway, but he drafted in reinforcements in the shape of Andrew Jones, the third partner, and together they managed to deal with most of the calls fairly quickly.

She went over to help get the children off to school and was told he was in bed asleep.

After Claire and Will had left, she went up with a cup of tea and woke him.

He was less than grateful, but after the night he had endured hard on the heels of the flood, she felt he was entitled to be a little grouchy.

She took Sophie to school and went back to check that he was up.

He was, slumped in the kitchen, coffee in hand, his eyes half closed.

She sat down opposite him and eyed him dispassionately. 'You look terrible.'

'Thank you. It's pretty bad from this side too.'

'I'm sure. Why don't you have a day off?'

He laughed. 'Because it doesn't go away. I expect the surgery's awash with gastric flu victims this morning, and probably my first job will be to mend the cistern in the loo. It always packs up under duress.'

'Have you eaten?'

He peered at her under bruised-looking lids. 'Are you a sadist or what?' he growled. 'No, I haven't bloody well eaten. I can't remember when I last ate.'

'Right — go and have a shower and I'll cook you something — go on, hurry, or you'll be late.'

He grumbled off upstairs while she whipped up some scrambled eggs and toast, and made a fresh pot of tea. He drank far too much coffee anyway.

Just as she dished up he reappeared, washed and dressed and looking almost human. She regretted the passing of the stubble on his jaw, though. It had lent him a rakish, piratical air that was somehow very attractive. . .

'Michael's all right, by the way.'

'Michael? Oh, Michael. Good.'

Gideon eyed her strangely, and she gulped down the last of her tea and stood up.

'I ought to get on. You eat that and I'll tell your patients you've been held up on a call and you'll be in shortly.'

'Lies, damn lies and statistics,' he mumbled.

'It isn't altogether a lie ——'

'Just the truth manipulated. Tell them what you like — I'm past caring.'

'Never mind — you can have an early night tonight,' she told him.'

'Wonderful,' he mumbled.

It was not to be.

At two in the afternoon the wind, which had been gusting all day, suddenly picked up and began to gust at well over a hundred miles an hour.

There were warnings from the Meteorological Office about driving and going out and about in such conditions, and Beth went to collect Sophie from school in the car to give them some protection from flying debris.

By this time the wind was blowing in earnest, and Beth parked outside and had to hold the railings to get into the school grounds safely.

Just as she was going in, there was a terrible tearing sound and a great section of the roof of the building lifted off and flew past her.

She could hear children screaming inside, and ran in.

'You'd better get out, the walls could go,' she yelled at the terrified teacher, and together they shepherded the little ones out to their frantic mothers.

As the crowd dispersed and the children were hurried home to safety, Beth noticed that the walls were beginning to sag.

'Look out!' she screamed, and then a whole section of

wall gave way and caved in on the few remaining children.

She didn't stop to think. There were children buried under there, and they had to be got out and fast.

'Call for help,' she shouted.

One mother who knew Sophie well said she'd take her home with her own daughter, but Jan Driscoll, from the Stop Smoking clinic, pitched in beside Beth, white-faced.

'You shouldn't be doing this,' Beth yelled at her.

'My son's in there,' she said grimly. 'Don't tell me what I can and can't do!'

Beth laid a hand on her arm and squeezed briefly. 'Just be careful.'

There was no reply, just a chin jutted in determination and hands pulling frantically at the rubble.

Help arrived, men with strong hands and equipment, and Gideon was amongst them.

'Where's Sophie?' he asked, his face a mask.

'She's fine — gone home with Mrs Blundle.'

His face flickered, and he nodded. 'OK. Let's get these children out.'

Three of the five trapped children had already been freed but two, including Mrs Driscoll's son, remained unaccounted for.

One last child, a girl, was brought out alive but unconscious, but there was no sign of the Driscoll boy.

'Oh, God, where is he? Jeremy!' she screamed, and Beth took her arm.

'Listen! I can hear him!'

Far away, beyond the howling of the wind, they heard a little boy crying, 'Mummy!'

Gideon vaulted over the pile of rubble, dived into the

ruins of the building and moments later emerged with young Jeremy Driscoll.

'He was in the loo—he's fine, just too terrified to come out. Take him home,' Gideon instructed, and Jan Driscoll turned away, her son in her arms, her bleeding hands wrapped around his shaking little body, and took him home.

They went to fetch Sophie from the Blundles, and, after taking her back to the house and making sure she was all right, Gideon took Beth back to the surgery and dressed her hands.

'They'll be fine in a couple of days, but you'd better rest them for now.'

'But what about the kids?' she asked.

The surgery was full of children covered in cuts and bruises, some with suspected fractures, others just badly frightened.

'You can stay and talk to them and do a little Triage for me, if you like, but I'm sure Julie can manage.'

Julie, however, was stricken with the tummy bug and so Beth, for all her damaged hands, put on a pair of large gloves over the dressings and carried on.

Her fingers were stiff and sore by the time they finished, and Gideon drove her home.

The local TV stations had sent camera crews over to film their frantic efforts at the school and together they sat down in the drawing-room and watched themselves at work.

'I wonder who alerted them?' Beth mused.

'Mabel Robinson, I expect,' he said drily, and she laughed.

He gave her a weary smile, and she reached out and

cupped his cheek. 'So much for your early night — it's already nine-thirty.'

'I feel wired,' he said quietly. 'I should be ready to sleep, but I feel — I don't know ——'

'I do. I feel the same. Why don't you walk me home and come in for a cup of cocoa?'

'Sure?' he asked. 'It's late and you're shattered.'

'I'm sure. I won't sleep yet.'

Not while I'm still trying to work out what those women on Monday night meant about you bringing up a cuckoo, she thought. Would he tell her if she asked? Probably not, but they had to have been talking about Sophie.

The others were too much like him, but Sophie with her mop of blonde curls and bright blue eyes was, indeed, a cuckoo — unless she took after the mother? Somehow Beth thought not. There was no doubting the love he felt for her, though. Beth had seen the worry in his eyes when he arrived at the school and saw the collapsed wall, and the hug he had given the little girl when they picked her up was enough to crack her ribs.

They went up to the flat and she put some milk on while Gideon prowled restlessly round, picking things up and putting them down again.

His face was drawn and he looked exhausted, but she knew it was no use suggesting he relax.

She handed him his cocoa, and he took her other hand and pulled her down onto the sofa beside him.

'Thanks for helping,' he murmured.

She laughed softly. 'Why thank me? I didn't do anything for you, or anything anybody else didn't do.'

'But they aren't your kids.'

'They aren't yours either. Sophie was out of there.'

She wondered if he would pick up on that, but he didn't. Instead he took her hand and smoothed the bandages on the back.

'Your poor hands. They're so soft — too soft for shifting rubble. You were wonderful on Monday, too.'

She laughed a little self-consciously. 'Everyone was. Even Mabel Robinson was helping.'

'Mabel never misses a get-together,' he said, 'and anyway, I was talking about Michael.'

'Where is he?'

'With his parents. It'll be ages before his cottage will be sorted out.'

He yawned, and set his cocoa down. 'Anyway,' he said with a smile, 'I think what I was really saying was, thank you for being you.'

He took her mug from her hand, placed it on the table and pulled her into his arms.

His lips were warm and firm, his kiss undemanding — at least at first. Then something shifted, and with a deep groan he threaded his hands through her hair to steady her as his mouth plundered hers.

'Damn, Beth, I want you,' he groaned, and she arched up against him, her body liquid fire under his hands.

She slid her arms round him and her fingers found a way under his jumper. She moaned in frustration as she realised she couldn't feel his skin through the bandages on her hands.

'What's wrong?' he murmured.

'I want to touch you but I can't feel anything,' she fretted. 'Oh, damn. . .'

A shudder ran through him as she stroked her hands

down his burning flesh, and the kiss ran wild, hot open-mouthed caresses that traced the line of her jaw, down over the hollow of her throat and on ——

'Take this off,' he growled, yanking at her jumper.

She sat up and stripped it over her head, and he reached for her again, almost tearing her shirt open in his haste.

'Oh, yes — I knew they'd be pink,' he gritted unsteadily, just as his head descended and he took one aching nipple into his mouth.

As he sucked she arched against him with a cry, and he lifted his head and stared at her, his eyes burning.

'Oh, God, what are we doing, Beth?' he whispered raggedly.

She reached out a hand and cupped his face. 'I don't know what you're doing, but I rather thought I was making love.'

A shudder ran through him and he straightened away from her, jerking to his feet and striding to the window to stand staring out into the night.

Slowly she stood up and pulled her shirt front together, then walked over to him and laid a hand against his back.

'Gideon?'

'It's crazy — it's late, we've got to work tomorrow, we're both exhausted from nights of broken sleep — it's no time to make a decision like this, Beth.'

'Is that a no?'

He sighed and stabbed his fingers through his hair. 'Hell, woman, don't do that to me.'

'Why?'

'Why? Because it isn't fair.'

'To who?' she asked blankly. 'Gideon, I want this to happen.'

He turned slowly, his eyes burning into hers.

'You're sure?'

She nodded. 'Certain.'

'Not like this,' he argued. 'Not when we're tired and dirty.'

'When, then?' she persisted. 'Tomorrow? The next day?'

He took a breath. 'This weekend. The children are all away, Will on a course, the girls to my parents. I'm on duty Friday night, but from twelve on Saturday I'm free.'

She gave him a tentative smile. 'Is that meant to give us both a cooling-off period, because if it is, I don't think it's going to work.'

He gave a wry snort and pulled her into his arms. 'Somehow I think you're right. However, just in case, we'll try it. And now I'm going, before I do something I regret.'

'You haven't had your cocoa yet.'

He glanced at the table and gave a short, hollow laugh. 'I'll pass on the cocoa. Who knows, it might keep me awake.'

She laughed softly. 'You mean you've been sleeping?'

He groaned and pulled her hard against him, lowering his mouth to hers for one last, searing kiss.

'Don't tease. I'm off.'

'You keep saying that.'

He released her slowly, his eyes touched with humour and firmly banked desire, and then turning on his heel he walked swiftly across the room and down the stairs.

'Goodnight, Beth,' he said softly. 'Sweet dreams.'

They weren't sweet — far from it — but they were filled with him, and those lovely grey-green eyes that burned into her soul.

The weekend seemed a terribly long way ahead.

CHAPTER SIX

As THE weekend drew closer, Beth found her apprehension growing.

Did he really want her? Or was she just convenient? Could she just as easily have been any other woman?

She didn't know, and there was no way she could find out short of asking him, and she certainly had no intention of doing that!

On Friday afternoon she collected Sophie from the church hall which had been pressed into use as a temporary school, and got her things ready for going away.

William had gone already on his school trip, and Claire had packed her things the night before, and they were stacked in the hall.

She was upstairs looking for Sophie's rabbit when she heard the doorbell ring, and seconds later Claire's voice as she answered the door.

'Hi, Grannie—come in. Beth's just sorting Sophie's stuff out—she won't be long. Sophie's watching telly. Cup of tea?'

'That would be lovely, darling.'

She heard their footsteps crossing the hall to the kitchen as she foraged in the laundry basket in the bathroom. It was the only place left to look.

She drew a blank, but as she came out on to the landing Claire's voice drifted up to her. 'Oh, she's great! Sophie adores her, and Dad—well, you should see the

way he looks at her when he thinks no one's looking!
I'm surprised she doesn't burst into flames!'

'Claire!'

'Well, it's true, Grannie. Wouldn't it be great if they
got married? She's really ace — something happened a
while ago and she really understood — she was brilliant — oh, I love her to death!'

'But does your father?'

Beth, frozen on the landing, waited breathlessly for
the reply.

'I don't know — he must, surely? How could he fail?
Anyway, he certainly fancies her ——'

'Claire, that's a disgusting expression.'

'So is the one on his face when he's looking at her — as
if he could eat her.'

'Claire! Really, that's enough! You don't know what
you're talking about.'

There was silence for a second, then Claire said
quietly, 'You're wrong, Grannie. I do know — and
what's wrong with it? It's years since Mum died, and
there hasn't been anyone. Don't you think it's time?'

There was another pause, followed by a sigh. 'Probably, but it's not for you to decide for them, darling.
Here, drink your tea.'

Beth backed quietly away from the top of the stairs
and went into Gideon's room.

Did he look at her as if he could eat her? She glanced
at the bed, and a shiver ran over her. She would be
there soon — probably tomorrow night. He had implied
he wanted to get tonight out of the way, but from
lunchtime tomorrow. . .

Her heart hammered against her ribs, and she licked

her dry lips and closed her eyes, forbidden images clothing the inside of her lids.

She heard footsteps on the stairs and the door opened and closed softly.

'Beth?'

She opened her eyes and turned towards him, still in a daze. 'Hi. Sophie's lost her rabbit.'

'It's here, she left it on my bed this morning.'

It was sitting on his pillow, one ear flopped tiredly over an eye, watching them. She picked it up. 'Your mother's in the kitchen with Claire.'

'Yes, I saw them. I think she's in a hurry.'

'Mmm.' Beth headed for the door, the rabbit clutched against her chest as if to hide her hammering heart. 'I didn't think you'd get home in time to see them.'

'I've got to go out in a minute, I've got surgery and a list of calls already.'

'What shall I do about your supper?' she asked, struggling for practicalities.

'Leave it in the oven — I'll get it when I come in.' He paused on the landing and drew her into his arms. 'I'll see you tomorrow — we'll have lunch together and go out somewhere in the afternoon. OK?'

She nodded, and he cupped her face and kissed her longingly. 'It's going to be a hell of a long night,' he whispered.

'Perhaps you'll be busy so you won't have time to think,' she said with a smile.

'If so I'll just be too tired to do you justice. Oh, God. . .' His eyes drifted shut and he sighed. 'Why aren't I an accountant or something normal, so I don't have to work tonight?'

'You wouldn't be the same person,' she told him, and

with a grin he took her arm and they headed down the stairs.

As they reached the hall the girls came out of the kitchen, followed by Gideon's mother who gave Beth a searching look.

'Mother, this is Beth Turner who's helping us out for a while. Beth, my mother.'

She took Mrs Pendragon's warm, capable hand and forced herself to meet those piercing grey eyes.

'So you're Beth. Claire's been telling me all about you.'

Beth, who knew exactly what Claire had been saying, flushed slightly. 'I hope it was good,' she flannelled.

'Oh, yes, my dear. Very good. Right, girls, let's away. Will you pick them up on Sunday night, Gideon?'

'Yes—sixish?'

'Make it four-thirty—you can come for high tea—and bring Beth. Rupert would love to meet her, I'm sure.'

Stunned, Beth watched them go. So Mrs Pendragon was going to vet her, was she?

She wondered what Gideon would say if he were privy to the conversation she had overheard.

'I must go,' he said now from beside her. 'I'll see you tomorrow.'

His eyes burned into her, and then he turned and ran lightly down the steps to his car. With a brief wave, he was gone and she went back into the house, her heart pounding.

Tomorrow. . .

Tomorrow, in fact, didn't go quite according to plan—at least at first. Beth was in the kitchen preparing lunch for them when the phone rang. It was Gideon, and he asked if she could go to the surgery and help him with some suturing.

'It's a friend of Claire's — Annabel. She's cut her hand badly — drawn a knife across the inside of all her fingers.'

'I'll be right over.'

She didn't bother to change, just washed her hands and put on her coat and walked briskly around to the surgery.

Molly directed her to the room used for minor surgical cases, and she went in and found Gideon with a girl of Claire's age and an agitated woman, clearly her mother.

'I just can't understand how you can have been so careless,' the mother was saying.

'My hand slipped.'

Beth glanced at the girl's drawn face. Behind the obvious pain was a certain mutinous withdrawal, as though she had no intention of discussing this accident with anyone, and most particularly not her mother.

Gideon ushered the woman out of the room while he did the suturing, and Beth assisted quietly, watching the girl as he worked.

Every finger was cleanly sliced, as if she had laid a knife in her hand, closed her fist and pulled the knife out sharply.

'Will it be permanently damaged?' Annabel asked after a while.

'No, I don't think so, but you won't be able to play in the Suffolk Festival this week, I'm afraid.'

Beth wasn't sure, but she thought she saw relief flicker over the girl's impassive features.

'How long will it take to heal?'

'Oh—several weeks. You managed to miss the tendons and there's no drastic nerve damage, but the muscles are all badly cut. It will take quite a bit of patience and perseverance before you get all your skills back on the piano, I'm afraid.'

'Doesn't matter,' the girl said quietly. 'Just so long as it's not permanent.'

Gideon and Beth exchanged glances over the girl, and without a word he finished tying off the last suture and straightened up. 'OK, Sister Turner, could you dress that for me, please? I'll go and have a word with your mother, Annie.'

He went out and left them alone together.

'Will it be very sore?' she asked, looking down at the row of sutures like little spiders marching across her fingers.

'Probably fairly tender for a day or two. You'd better keep it dry—I'll spray some plastic skin on in case you get it wet, and just put a light dressing on to keep it clean.'

The girl sighed, and Beth decided to take the risk.

'Why did you do it, Annie?'

Her eyes flew up, startled, and locked with Beth's, then slid away. 'Who says I did?'

Beth shrugged and carried on working. 'You don't have to tell me if you don't want to, and I wouldn't tell your mother. It's just that when young people do something like this to themselves, it's usually a cry for help. If someone doesn't recognise that, it's really all rather a waste of time, isn't it?'

Slowly, great tears welled in her eyes and spilt over her cheeks.

'I just wanted some time to myself — time when I didn't have to play the damn piano! I used to love it when it was just for fun, but my new teacher — she thinks I could make a career out of it, and she's pushing me. Mum and Dad want me to do it, too, and they're paying a fortune for this special tuition, and I just hate it now —'

She broke off, too upset to carry on, and Beth put her arms round her and rocked her gently.

'There, there, love — it's all right. You'll be OK, don't worry. Do you want Dr Pendragon to talk to you mother, try and help her to understand how you feel?'

Annabel straightened up, her eyes wide. 'She'll kill me!' she whispered.

'No, she won't. She loves you. Give her a chance to prove it.'

After a long, thoughtful moment she nodded. 'OK.'

'Good girl — you stay where you are and I'll finish this and go and talk to him.'

She found them in his office, the mother in tears, Gideon patiently explaining that too much pressure could easily tip children over the brink, particularly if they were sensitive and gifted, like Annabel.

'Could I have a word?' she asked softly.

He came to the door and pulled it to behind him. 'What is it?'

'She did it — she told me. They've got her a new teacher and she's been put under much more pressure. She says she hates it now, and it used to be fun. She just wanted some time to herself.'

He sighed. 'Mrs Steel doesn't believe me.'

'Well, she'd better because that poor kid is perched on a knife edge — literally.'

He nodded. 'I'll sort it out. You go on back and leave it with me now. I've got two calls to make and I'll be home.'

Home, she thought as she made her way back.

It had a lovely ring to it. She wondered if it would ever be their home and not just his.

She was in the kitchen when he came in, putting the finished touches to their lunch.

She turned towards him, wiping her hands on a towel, and met his eyes. What would he say? How would he behave?

She felt suddenly terribly inexperienced and ill-equipped to deal with a relationship with Gideon. After all he had a very full life — was there room for her in it? Suddenly she doubted it.

'Lunch is ready,' she said as calmly as she could manage, and looked away, unable to cope with that measured stare.

'Do you want lunch?' he asked quietly.

She glanced back, drawn by something in his voice, and met such a look of naked longing that it took her breath away.

She shook her head. 'No — no, I don't want lunch.'

'Good,' he growled softly, 'because neither do I.'

He held out his hand, and she slipped hers into it. Without a word he led her towards the stairs and up to his room.

The door closed behind them with a decisive click, and she swallowed. He was standing behind her, not touching her, and yet she could feel his eyes boring into her back.

She stood like a statue, unable to move, and then she

felt his hands at the nape, loosening her hair and fanning it out over her shoulders.

'Take off your clothes,' he said gruffly. 'I want to see you.'

Panic flooded her. What if he didn't like what he saw? She was too thin, she knew that, and her breasts were small — Her lids fluttered down. What if she couldn't please him?

'Beth?'

His voice was soft, little more than a whisper, and she turned towards him.

His eyes were like hot coals, raging with desire, and yet she sensed his hesitation.

Was he thinking the same as her? It was quite possible, she supposed.

'Please,' he said. 'Let me see you.'

His voice was gruff, almost pleading, and Beth heard in it a trace of desperation.

Lord, how she wanted him — not just now, not just like this, but for ever, always, to have and to hold, from this day forward. . .

How would he know that unless she showed him? And how would she know if he returned her feelings unless she gave him the chance?

Her courage returned, and with it an instinct for arousal that she didn't know she possessed.

She would make him want her, want her so much that he was helpless to deny himself. He needed her — all she had to do was show him that.

She stripped slowly, taking her time with the buttons on her blouse, unfastening it and then turning her attention to her shoes, allowing the edges of the blouse to fall open as she bent forward.

She heard the sharp intake of his breath and straightened, hitching the shoes off with the toe of the other foot, her eyes on his face.

She reached for the zip of her jeans and slid it down, the sound rasping over the nerve-endings, leaving them tingling.

Gideon's chest rose and fell sharply as she slid them down her legs and straightened, kicking them away.

Then she turned from him and slipped off the blouse, then the bra.

She left the tiny scrap of lace that passed for bikini briefs, and dropping her head forward slightly so her hair draped over her shoulders and covered her breasts, she turned back towards him.

'Your turn,' she said huskily.

He was too impatient for her delicate striptease routine. Instead he yanked off his tie, tossed it aside and pulled his shirt over his head.

Her breath lodged in her throat. He was beautiful — strong, lean, supple, the dark hair tangled across the centre of his chest, arrowing down ——

His fingers were there now, struggling with the hook on his trousers, then it was free and the zip was down and he was yanking them off, kicking his shoes aside as he went.

Like her, he left the briefs, but he might as well not have bothered. They weren't designed to contain such powerful reactions.

For an age they stood, their gazes locked, and then Gideon held out his hand.

She reached up and took it, and he reeled her in, wrapping his arms around her and crushing her against his chest.

She felt the soft scrape of those dark curls against her nipples, and her breath punched out of her on a wordless gasp. Her name fluttered in her hair, soft puffs of his breath teasing against her skin.

She lifted her hands, now free of their bandages, and laid them against the hot satin of his back.

He jerked at the contact, his control drawn so taut he could scarcely stand it.

She knew that because when he had touched her in the same way, her body had jerked too, as if he had some secret access to her strings. He had scarcely touched her and yet she felt drawn tighter than a bow.

'Please,' she breathed. 'Gideon, please. . .'

He lifted her effortlessly against his chest and set her down in the centre of the huge four-poster bed that had hosted all her dreams.

Then he stretched out beside her, his body quivering, and almost reverently framed her face with his trembling hands.

'I want you so badly I'm afraid I'll hurt you.'

She reached up and cupped his cheek. 'You won't hurt me—I need you, too,' she whispered, and drew his face down for her kiss.

The first touch of his mouth on hers shattered the slender threads of their control. Their loving was wild, untamed, almost primitive in its passion, and when she felt herself shatter and start to fall, he was with her, his cry muffled by her hair, his body shuddering under her hands.

After an age he lifted himself up and looked down at her, his fingers brushing her cheek.

'You cried,' he said, wonder in his voice. 'Did I hurt you?'

She shook her head. 'No. It was just——' She shrugged, unable to put it into words, and he hugged her gently and curled her into his side.

'I know.'

They slept then, waking later to make love again.

As he lay beside her, his hand cupping one breast, his thumb grazing the soft rose-pink nipple, he murmured, 'I can just see you, your hair flowing round your shoulders like a shawl, a baby at your breast.'

Pain stabbed through her, taking her breath away. Oh, lord, she thought she was over it. . .

Her stiffness must have registered with him, because he turned his head and met her eyes, his own worried. 'Beth—I know this is hardly the time to think of contraception, but——'

'It's OK,' she said flatly. 'I'm on the Pill.'

His shoulders sagged. 'Thank God. I can't believe I was so irresponsible.'

She stared up at the ceiling, still devastated by the pain his words had caused. Her breasts ached for that greedy little mouth, and the yearning low down in her abdomen was so real it was almost physical. 'Would a baby be so awful?' she asked shakily.

He snorted. 'Are you kidding? I've got three children already, Beth. The last thing I need is any more.'

She ignored this extra little dart of pain. There was no certainty of their future yet—perhaps there never would be. To even consider a baby now was the height of irresponsibility, and yet—no, she couldn't turn the clock back, couldn't find again what she had already lost. It would only salve the wound.

Something in her stillness must have alerted him, because he lifted himself on one elbow and stared down at her, his eyes concerned. His hand came up and brushed her cheek tentatively.

'Beth? What is it? Tell me.'

'I had a miscarriage,' she told him, her voice quiet and curiously flat. 'Two years ago. I'd known him a few months — he was a partner in another group practice close to ours. They did reciprocal duties. When I told him I was pregnant, he was appalled. It appeared he was already married with two children, and my condition was just an embarrassment.' She looked at him. 'Matthew wanted me to have an abortion, and when I refused he went off at the deep end and hit me. I lost the baby — a girl — at sixteen weeks.' She closed her eyes, the pain of memory too great to share. 'He went to Australia, and two months ago he came back.'

She laughed, a strained, unnatural laugh. 'He even had the nerve to look me up.'

'Is that why you ran away?'

She met his eyes then. 'I didn't run. I walked. Call it cowardice or self-preservation, call it what you like. I just had to be away from him. He'd hurt me enough. He no longer had the power to hurt me, but just seeing him left a bitter taste in my mouth. That's why I'm on the Pill — so it can never, ever happen again.'

Gideon was silent for a while, then he leant down and kissed her, just once, very gently.

'I'm sorry.'

She swallowed. 'How could he? How could he want his child to die? How could he be unfaithful to his wife? I just didn't understand.'

Gideon lay down and took her hand, threading his fingers through hers.

'I didn't, either. Denise did it to me for years before

she left me. Claire was an attempt at reconciliation, but when she was four Denise met someone else, and went without leaving so much as a note. Four years later she was back, pregnant, hungry and homeless. I took her back — what choice did I have? She was still my wife, the mother of my children, the mother of their sibling. She died in childbirth — a post-partum haemorrhage. My mother said it was poetic justice. I'm afraid to say I was simply relieved that it was all over.'

'Do the children know?'

'Know what?'

'That Sophie isn't your child.'

'She is my child — in everything but genetics, she's mine. My name's on her birth certificate.' He sighed. 'But yes, they know — everyone knows. In a village as intimate as Barnham Market you can't keep a secret, especially not a juicy one like that. Besides, she's nothing like me or Denise, so it was fairly obvious.'

'She's a lovely little girl.'

'Mmm. I know. I love her very dearly.'

'I know you do. You love them all very much, don't you? It can't have been very easy.'

He laughed, a parody of a laugh that made her want to hold him and take away the long, lonely years.

'Easy? Hell, no, it hasn't been easy, but it has its rewards.'

'They're a credit to you, Gideon.'

He turned his head and smiled at her. 'You're a lovely girl, Beth, do you know that?'

She laughed softly. 'Don't, you'll make me blush.'

'Good — you're beautiful when you blush.'

She blushed then, just to oblige him, and he hugged her closer and dropped a kiss on her forehead.

'Do you know what I want to do now?'

She lifted herself up and looked down at him, her hair sweeping across his chest like a silken curtain. 'No, what?'

'God, I've had dreams about you doing that,' he groaned, and threading his fingers through her hair, he sifted it slowly through them, his eyes glazed. 'You are so, so lovely.' His eyes locked with hers, and he pulled her down against his chest and pressed his lips to hers in a tender kiss devoid of passion.

She lifted her head and looked at him, studying his face, the deep creases around his eyes, the laughter lines bracketing his mouth. 'You never told me what you want to do now,' she murmured lazily.

She ran a finger over his lip and he opened his mouth and nipped it gently.

'Guess.'

Just then his stomach rumbled loudly and she giggled. 'Eat?'

'You got it in one. I'm starving. Can we have lunch?'

'Mmm. It's a salad — it's ready when we are.'

He chuckled. 'You must have known.'

'Just hedging my bets,' she said with a satisfied smile.

Throwing off the bedclothes he bounded off the bed and flung her his towelling robe. 'Here, wear that. I'll sling on my jeans.'

He did, looking impossibly sexy with bare feet, no shirt and the zip yanked up. The stud gaped revealingly, and Beth ached to run her fingers over the hard washboard of his stomach and tease the fine hair that arrowed under the zip ——

'Stop looking at me like that or you won't get your lunch,' he growled.

'Shame — it'll keep, you know.'

'Hussy. I need to eat to keep my strength up — and so do you. Come.'

He held out his hand, and she threaded her fingers through his and went down with him to the kitchen.

They never did make it out of the door that day, nor the next, not until the afternoon when they had to go to fetch the children.

'Do I really have to come?' Beth protested.

'Mmm. Royal command.'

She snorted. 'I hate being vetted.'

He turned and stared at her. 'Vetted? Why the hell should you be vetted?'

'Oh, come on — I'm virtually living with you and they know it. They want to be sure I'm good enough for their little boy.'

He made a rude noise. 'I'm forty-two, Beth. They stopped interfering in my social life years ago.'

'They did?' Beth said sceptically. 'We'll see.'

'You were right,' he said.

'I shan't say I told you so.'

He snorted rudely.

They were walking back to the coach house, a careful gap between them in case the children looked out of the window. She turned and poked her tongue out at him.

'And to you. You passed, by the way. Mother said you were lovely, and Dad said I had his permission to bring you into the family.' Gideon snorted again. 'He must be mad.'

Beth went still. 'Why?'

'Are you crazy? Why do I want any more responsibility? The kids are more than enough for anyone — the last thing I need is another wife.'

'Even if you found someone you loved?'

He looked at her then, and his eyes closed.

'Oh, no, Beth. Don't go imagining yourself in love with me, for God's sake.'

'Why?' she asked softly. 'Would it really be so very awful to be loved?'

His shoulders sagged, and he took her in his arms and rested his forehead against hers. 'Oh, Beth. It would be so easy to hold you like this and tell you that I love you, and pretend that everything was going to be sunshine and roses, but life's not like that. I'm torn three ways already, Beth. I can't cope with any more. There's just nothing left to give.'

She reached up and framed his face in her hands, willing him to see the love in her eyes.

'You could always take.'

'No.' He covered her hands with his and eased them away. 'Beth, I'm sorry. I know you're a roses-round-the-door happy-ever-after person, and if I've hurt you, I'm sorry, but I can't afford to get involved — and anyway, I'm years older than you. Hell, you're nearer William's age than you are mine.'

She swallowed her hurt. 'I didn't notice you exactly lagging behind this weekend.'

He flushed. 'Don't. We mustn't do it again.'

'Why?'

'Because you're only here for a short while, and when you leave it'll just hurt you more.'

She gave him a long, level look. 'Is that what you're really afraid of? Me being hurt? Or are you afraid you'll fall in love with me, and when I leave, you'll hurt every bit as much as I do?'

He stared at her, his face a mask, then dropping his hands he stepped away.

'Gideon, it doesn't have to be like this,' she told him softly.

'It does. Please, Beth, don't make it any worse — for either of us. There's no future for us. Don't ask me for promises.'

'All right, I won't. Just six months of your life.'

'No!'

'Gideon, it's too late for regrets. We're going to have the pain — we may as well have the joy first.'

He stiffened his resolve. 'No, Beth, we can't. People will talk. We can't hide it, and then the children will get wind of it and expect us to get married, and it's just out of the question. All we'll end up doing is hurting the kids, and I won't do that, Beth — not for me, not for anybody.'

She drew a steadying breath and straightened her shoulders. 'You're right. I wouldn't want to hurt them either. But. . .'

Her eyes filled, and he reached for her.

'Oh, God,' he groaned, and then she was in his arms, crushed against his chest. 'I didn't mean to hurt you,' he breathed. 'I never meant to bring you pain. Forgive me.'

She smoothed her hands down his back and held him close. 'There's nothing to forgive. Just take what you want from me, give what you can, and live for now. If you can give me nothing else, Gideon, give me memories.'

'No, Beth — please. I can't.' His arms tightened, and

then he released her, pressing a hard, desperate kiss to her lips before turning and striding quickly away.

She watched him go, then went up to her flat and showered, changed into her nightdress, climbed into bed and cried herself to sleep.

CHAPTER SEVEN

GIDEON was miserable

This morning Claire had refused to co-operate with him, maintaining that he didn't love her or understand her and flouncing off to the bus stop in tears.

Gideon always found scenes like that frustratingly painful. His love for his children was the driving force of his life, and the hurt when they denied it was out of all proportion to reason. He knew they were just saying it — just as he knew this morning that Claire was simply expressing her frustration in the only way she could.

But it hurt — God, it hurt. Logically he realised they knew he loved them — of course they did — but today, just to make things worse, she had flung Beth in his face.

'*She* understands me — why can't you marry her and then there'll be *someone* in this miserable family who cares about me?'

He had been trying hard not to think about Beth — an impossibility since his sheets were rich with her fragrance and his dreams had been full of her image.

The dreams had changed.

Instead of scenes of wild passion — which paled into insignificance in the face of the real Beth — he had seen her face shimmering and fading, and he had tried to run after her and stop her going, only to find his legs wouldn't work properly.

He had woken sweating and trembling, and as the

dream receded he had dragged his hand over his face and collapsed back on to the pillows. Her scent asailed him, the delicate fragrance curling round his senses and torturing him.

In the end he had slept again, and this morning they had been on the drag, Sophie tired after her weekend away, Claire stubborn and unrelenting.

And now he was at work, hiding in his room, pretending that everything was all right.

He didn't know how to face Beth. Her eyes last night had been luminous with hurt, but he couldn't afford involvement — could he?

Even now, thinking about it brought a tightness to his chest and set his pulse racing. The children were more than enough. To have responsibility for Beth's happiness as well was more than he could cope with.

He pressed the buzzer for his next patient and picked up the notes.

It was Brian Hurley who had had a piece of wood removed from his hand a week ago in the flood. As he unwrapped the dressing Gideon could see that the wound was still angry and inflamed, although he had been on antibiotics. The man was generally feeling well, and Gideon suspected that there was an abscess forming in the wound, perhaps due to a tiny residue of splinter left deep in the ball of his thumb.

'Are you back in the bungalow yet?' he asked as he examined it.

'No — waiting for the insurance money so we can go and buy new carpets and furniture. Lost the lot in the end, even the kitchen units. Chipboard, of course — acts like a sponge when you give it a good soak. Ouch!'

'Sorry. Look, I think I'd like Sister Turner to take the

stitch out and dress it, and we'll just leave it open for a while to see if the poison will come out.'

He stood up and opened the door, and escorted the man down the corridor to Beth's room.

The door was open and she was just going into the waiting-room for the next patient.

'Ah, Sister Turner, could you spare me a minute?'

She turned slowly, and Gideon's heart seemed to swell in his chest.

She looked tired, but more than that. There was a haunted quality about her, and she didn't quite meet his eyes.

That hurt. After all they had shared. . .

'Could you take the stitch out and have a look at this? It might do better just left to drain. Perhaps some antibiotic spray into the wound if it hasn't closed, and a regular dressing change—can you come in every day, Mr Hurley?'

'Suppose so—can't work with it like this.'

'No, of course not. I'll write you a sick note and leave it in Reception—you can collect it on your way out. Thank you, Sister.'

Beth nodded. 'You're welcome,' she said quietly.

He turned away. It was ridiculous. She wanted their relationship to carry on, and if he was honest, so did he—so why not?

Because you'll end up hurting her, he told himself.

And you haven't already? a little voice needled.

He smiled absently at a patient in the corridor and went into his room, closing the door firmly.

Damn. He couldn't bear to see her hurting. With a sigh he collapsed into his chair and stared blankly out of the window. As a doctor he had had to learn that there were times when pain was a necessary part of the healing process. Sometimes that pain had to be inflicted.

He knew that.

So why couldn't he be philosophical about Beth?

Beth collected Sophie from the church hall after school and took her back to the house — she refused to call it home — and they got a drink and a biscuit and curled up together on the settee in the breakfast room and looked at her reading book.

As they read the page together, Beth tried hard to think about something other than the warmth of the little body snuggled against her side, the fragrance of those soft, bouncy curls that teased her chin, the bright little eyes that turned up to her, full of mischief and laughter.

Thinking about Sophie and how much she loved her was counter-productive. Anyway, Beth didn't think there was room for any more pain.

Will came back on the bus with Claire, complete with a mountain of filthy washing from his biology field trip.

'Good time?' she asked him.

He gave her a tired grin. 'Great — very muddy after all last week's rain. I'm sorry about the state of the clothes.'

She tried to smile, but it simply wouldn't come. He was so like his father. . .

'Beth? Are you OK?'

She nodded and turned quickly away, carrying his case through to the utility-room and putting things to soak before washing.

He followed her. 'Beth? What's wrong?'

She scrubbed the tears from her cheeks with the back

of her hand and shook her head. 'Nothing,' she told him, but she was unconvincing. Her voice was clogged with tears, and the cheeks she had just dried seemed to be wet again.

Gently, and a little awkwardly, Will put his arms round her and hugged her.

'Beth, don't,' he pleaded. 'Look, I'm sorry—I know they're muddy—I'll do it.'

She sniffed and turned her face up to his. 'Oh, Will— it's not your clothes!' Her face crumpled and she turned away again.

He let her go, too awkward to deal with her tears, and she pulled herself together and blew her nose.

'Sorry. Now, is there anything here you'll need for tomorrow for school?'

He shook his head, clearly bemused. 'No. I've got other stuff.'

She nodded. 'Right—chicken for supper, OK?'

'Fine. Um, I've got work to do from the field trip— are you sure you're OK?'

She nodded again, and braved a smile. It couldn't have been too wobbly, because he looked reassured and picked up his school-bag and went upstairs to his room.

Seconds later Guns 'n' Roses were making the windows shake.

It was the last of the main course of Stop Smoking clinics. There would be follow-ups, in two weeks and two months, and they would be welcome to drop in to subsequent clinics for a little positive reinforcement.

Beth wondered if there was a clinic where she could go to help overcome her addiction to Gideon.

Not that there seemed to be any danger of being

allowed any further access to him, except in the most correct and professional capacity.

He had been politely distant this morning when he brought Mr Hurley along, and although she hadn't looked at him, she had no doubt that his face was quite impassive.

Years of training at hiding his feelings, she supposed, and swallowed the lump in her throat.

The patients arrived and Gideon came in seconds later — a carefully timed entrance to avoid any unwarranted contact, she thought cynically.

There was one notable absentee — Paul Stone.

'Don't think you'll be seeing him again,' one of the women told them. 'He's back on it hard as he can go — I saw him the other day outside the shop, and he had a packet in his hand then.'

'The flood caused such a lot of damage to his crops,' David Hendry commented. 'I saw him in the pub the other night, drowning his sorrows — terrible mess, he said. Worse than he thought at first. He's going to plough the whole lot in and write it off.'

'This is one of the problems,' Gideon said. 'Stress hits us all from time to time, and if there's a weak spot, like smoking or drinking, we tend to give in to it under pressure. It's finding other safety valves that is the key to staying a non-smoker.'

'Or a more convincing reason to give up than to go on,' Jan Driscoll said. 'I had three the other night, after the school wall collapsed and I thought Jeremy was under it, then I thought to myself, "What's the point of smoking because I'm so relieved he's alive, if I'm just going to kill him and the baby off with the smoke?" So I stopped again.'

They all praised her, Gideon particularly who had experienced the same devastating fear and subsequent relief over Sophie.

It was about halfway through the clinic when Paul Stone appeared.

'Sorry to interrupt,' he said, 'only I thought it was rude to leave without thanking you for trying, and saying goodbye to everyone.'

'Why don't you stay now you're here?' Gideon said. 'Beth was just going to make a cup of coffee for us all.'

'Oh — all right then.' He looked a little uneasy, Beth thought as she headed for the kitchen.

She, on the other hand, was much more relaxed out of Gideon's immediate vicinity.

They finished the clinic with a re-run of the damage smoking could do to your health, the help that was available and massive congratulations for such a heroic effort.

Eight out of the original ten had succeeded, a percentage Beth had never equalled in London, and she had to attribute the difference to Gideon's infectious enthusiasm and almost religious zeal.

As they left she gave each of them a questionnaire asking how much they felt the course had helped them, and whether or not they would recommend it to others. They were asked to highlight areas which had been particularly good, and others where they felt more help could have been forthcoming, and requested to bring the form back with them when they returned in two weeks for the follow-up session.

Paul hung back until the others had gone, then tapped his leg nonchalantly with the form.

'Don't suppose there's a lot of point taking this,

really. I mean, people like me just mess up your figures, don't we?'

Beth smiled reassuringly at him. 'This isn't about figures, Paul—it's about helping you to make a change in your lifestyle.'

He sighed. 'Yeah, well—no point in coming back for the follow-up, I don't suppose.'

'Not unless you have another go in the meantime,' Gideon suggested quietly.

Paul met his eyes, startled. 'But I've failed.'

Gideon shook his head. 'No, you've lapsed. Do you still want to give up?'

'Oh, God, yes.'

'Then you haven't failed, because you're still trying, or intending to. And there's no time like the present.'

He pursed his lips and stared at the floor for a second, then seemed to make up his mind.

'Got a bin handy?' he asked.

Beth held up a waste-paper basket.

He reached into his pocket and pulled out a nearly new packet of cigarettes and a disposable gas lighter. He dropped them ceremoniously into the bin.

'Well done,' she said warmly, and he gave a gentle snort.

'We'll see—there's many a slip 'twixt cup and lip, and all that.'

'So you'll be back in a fortnight,' Gideon pushed cautiously.

He exhaled. 'Yes, I'll be back. I know it makes sense—I'm just weak.'

'If it helps, drug addicts on cocaine have been given intravenous nicotine and said it felt like cocaine— they've also said that smoking is harder to give up.'

Paul looked astonished. 'I thought it was bloody hard!'

Gideon laughed and slapped him affectionately on the back. 'Go on, go and give it another whirl. If you need more support, come in or ring us. We're always available.'

He went then, and Beth and Gideon were left in an awkward silence.

She busied herself stacking coffee-cups and packing up leaflets, and after a second he joined in and helped her, packing the stuff away into the cupboard while she took the cups through to the kitchen.

He followed her through, standing silently watching her while she quickly rinsed them out and stacked them on the draining-board.

'Beth?' he said softly.

She froze. 'What?'

After a long, aching moment there was a sigh. 'Nothing, I — forget it.'

He turned on his heel and walked away, and she dried her hands, picked up her coat and headed out of the door.

He followed her home, his solid footfalls louder than the light sound of her sensible working shoes.

She managed to stay ahead of him, turning quickly to the coach house and slipping through the door, shutting it firmly behind her.

Tears prickled in her eyes, but she ignored them. Once was enough in a single day. Hanging up her coat, she headed upstairs and found a box of chocolates nestling on her bed, a note attached.

'Sorry I made you cry — Will,' she read, and the tears she had meant to ignore flowed even faster.

'Oh, idiot boy, it wasn't you,' she sobbed, and falling on to the bed, she let herself cry.

'Will made Beth cry this afternoon,' Claire said coldly as he ate his lonely supper.

'What?' Gideon put down his knife and fork and looked across at his son. 'What the hell did you do?'

He shifted awkwardly. 'I don't know—I didn't make her cry, exactly. She just sort of started. I asked her if she was OK, and—well, she took my washing to do, and it was really muddy. I thought that was it, maybe, because she was sorting it out and putting it in to soak, and then all of a sudden there were all these tears.'

He looked completely baffled, and Claire was smugly victorious.

'I think it's you,' she told her father. 'I think she's crying because you did something to her over the weekend.'

Gideon fought the flush and stood up, pushing his plate away. 'I'll go and see her,' he muttered.

'I took her some chocs,' William offered. 'While she was at the surgery, I went up and put them on her bed.'

'You went into her flat?' Gideon yelled.

'What's wrong with that?' he yelled back. 'I knew she was out—I only took her a present, damn it. Hell, Dad, she goes in my room all the time; why is it so different?'

Gideon didn't know, he just knew that the idea of his son going into Beth's room to give her chocolates left an unpleasant taste in his mouth.

'Just don't do it again,' he growled now, and striding out of the kitchen, he yanked open the back door and slammed it behind him with a satisfying thud.

* * *

The imperious rap on the door startled Beth. She jumped to her feet, scattering chocolates everywhere, and ran downstairs to open it.

'Gideon! What a surprise.' She drew the edges of her dressing-gown together and forced herself to look at him.

He looked awful. His eyes trailed slowly over her, then wandered back to her face. 'Um — I'm sorry, I didn't realise you'd gone to bed.'

'I haven't — I just had a bath.' She was suddenly aware of her dishevelled state, her hair piled up haphazardly on top of her head, her face stripped of make-up and naked to his eyes, the ravages of her emotion clearly visible.

He searched her face, his eyes troubled. 'Will said you'd been crying,' he said gruffly.

Her eyes filled again. 'It was nothing.'

'I'm sorry he came into your flat — I've told him not to do it again.'

'Oh, you shouldn't — Gideon, I've got no secrets. He brought me chocolates to cheer me up.'

'And have they?'

She turned away. 'No. They made me cry again.'

Her name was like a prayer in the quiet of the hall. Slowly, her heart in her mouth, she turned back to him.

His face was tortured, racked with guilt and something else — need? She wanted to wrap her arms around him and hold him, but she couldn't. He had to make the first move; she had done enough.

Slowly, hesitantly, he lifted his hand and brushed the tears from her cheeks. 'Oh, Beth.'

Then she was in his arms, crushed against his chest,

and he was raining kisses down on her hair and murmuring words of comfort in her ear.

She tilted her face to his and their lips met and melded, clinging in desperation as they drank deeply from each other.

'Come to bed,' she said softly when he lifted his head.

He needed no encouragement. Lifting her easily into his arms he carried her up the spiral and laid her carefully in the centre of the bed. In seconds his clothes were gone and he was beside her, parting her dressing-gown and gazing longingly at her nakedness.

'I need you now,' he groaned, and she opened her arms, welcoming his weight as he lowered himself gently on to her.

'Oh, God, I can't —' he choked out, and then they were locked together, his hands trapping her head against the onslaught of his mouth as his body plunged into hers again and again, driving them both to a desperate, aching release.

As her heart slowed and her lungs grew more able to cope, she lifted one boneless hand and stroked it tenderly over his back.

'I love you,' she said, quite slowly and clearly. She didn't want there to be any misunderstandings.

'Beth, don't,' he groaned raggedly.

'It's true. I'm not going to lie to you, not even by omission.'

He lifted his head and stared at her, then his lids fluttered down and she felt his ribs heave with a sigh.

'I'm sorry,' he murmured into her hair. 'I shouldn't be here. It isn't fair. All day I've been tortured by your silence — knowing I've hurt you. Beth, I don't know what to say. . .'

She held him, knowing what she wanted to hear and knowing just as clearly that she wouldn't, not ever.

'Just hold me,' she said eventually, and he rolled to the side and wrapped her in his arms. Her head lay across his chest, and as she listened to the steady, even beat of his heart, he sifted her hair through his fingers and spread it across his chest like a golden cloak.

'I wish things could be different,' he said quietly. 'If I didn't have the children — if you didn't have to go away. . .'

'I don't have to,' she reminded him.

'You do. You know that — I know that.'

'Do the children know that?'

'Don't,' he muttered. 'Claire gave me stick this morning. Wanted me to marry you so that someone in our miserable family would love and understand her.'

'Oh, Gideon. . .' Her hand came up and cupped his cheek, and he turned his face and pressed a kiss into her palm.

'I do love her — I don't always understand her, but she knows I love her.'

'Of course she does, and so do the others. It's just standard adolescent jargon.'

Except, of course, when Beth had screamed the same accusation at her parents, it had been true. At least Gideon's children were loved and wanted. How wonderful it must be to come first in someone's life.

Her eyes threatened to fill again, and she blinked back the tears and lifted her head.

'Coffee?'

'Mmm — just a small one. I ought to get back really.'

She tugged the edge of her dressing-gown out from

under his hip and slid off the bed, pattering over to the kitchen area in bare feet.

He lay on the top of the quilt, hands locked behind his head, oblivious to his nakedness, and watched her as she scooped the chocolates off the floor and piled them back into the box.

'Here,' she said with a smile, 'have one of your son's chocolates.'

He scowled, and she came and sat beside him, amused.

'Why does it worry you so much? Is it that he came up here, or because he gave me chocolates?'

Gideon shrugged too casually. 'It doesn't worry me.'

Her smile widened. 'Liar,' she said softly, and fed him a caramel.

'How did you know I liked caramels?' he mumbled.

She grinned. 'I didn't, but there's no choice — it's a box of caramels.'

He eyed the box closely. 'That's my box! One of the patients gave me them last week! Cheeky little wretch!'

Beth collapsed against him, giggling helplessly. 'Oh, Gideon — oh, don't be cross with him, he means well. It was a sweet gesture, and I won't let you be angry with him about it.'

Gideon snorted, but she fed him another caramel and shut him up. While he freed his teeth for further argument she went and made the coffee and brought it back to bed, snuggling against his side while he wrapped one arm around her shoulders and hugged her closer.

They finished their coffee and she washed up the mugs while he pulled on his clothes, then with a last lingering kiss he left her.

She stopped him just as he was going. 'Gideon, what

happens now?' she asked. She didn't want to, but she had to know for the sake of her sanity.

'God knows,' he replied heavily. 'Nothing's changed.'

She gave a sad little smile. 'No, I don't suppose it has, has it?'

Will was waiting for him when he got in.

'How is she?' he asked without preamble.

He flushed guiltily. 'Um — OK, I think.'

'Did you manage to sort it out?'

He sighed and dropped into one of the kitchen chairs. 'I don't know. We ate some of my chocolates.'

It was William's turn to blush.

'Sorry — I just thought —— '

'I know what you thought, and it was a very kind gesture. She asked me to thank you.'

Father and son exchanged understanding smiles, the earlier harsh words forgotten.

Then William reached out and took his father's hand, turning it over and examining the long, strong fingers one by one. 'You know, it would solve so many of your problems if you married her —— '

Gideon snatched his hand back as if he had been bitten. 'Don't you start!' he growled, and, oblivious to the hurt expression on his son's face, he marched into his study and shut the door firmly.

William, confused and just a little sick of trying to make sense of the emotions of adults, helped himself to a huge bowl of ice-cream and took it up to his room.

Beth peeped through her curtains at the house just before she went to bed. The light was on in Gideon's study, and as she watched he came to the window and waved.

She blew him a kiss and watched as he blew one back, then with a last lingering glance she closed the curtains and climbed into bed.

Had anything changed? Probably not.

He was still as determined as ever that there could be no future for them, but now she felt more hopeful than she had last night. Then she was convinced he was just sorry because he had used her.

Tonight, somehow, had been different. She thought he was almost sorry that there could be nothing for them, as if the idea was appealing.

Only the children held him back, and for that she had to respect him.

How many men of his age with three children to bring up would turn away from a woman who had all but offered to look after them? Most men, she realised, would grab such a ready-made nanny and housekeeper with both hands, but not Gideon.

He was more concerned about not hurting her and the children, and not short-changing her because he thought he had nothing left to offer her.

If it hadn't been so sad, she would have laughed. Everything she had ever wanted was to be found under his roof, and more that she had never even dreamed of.

Her childhood had been a loveless desert, her emotional life as an adult fraught with false starts and tragic errors of judgement.

Gideon, she knew, was the only man she had ever met who could take away that legacy of pain and fill her life with love and laughter.

If, God forbid, she couldn't talk him round, she would never love again.

No one could ever take his place in her heart, and it wouldn't be fair to expect anyone to try.

No, he was her only chance of happiness, and she would have to fight for it.

After all, what did she have to lose?

CHAPTER EIGHT

FROM then on their relationship slipped into an easy routine. Beth stopped avoiding Gideon all the time, and when he was late home for supper she ate with him.

They often sat together until quite late in the evening, discussing patients and treatments, and he used her as a sounding-board for particularly difficult or painful cases.

Towards the end of that first week he was on call on the Thursday night, and tapped on her door on his way home.

'Mabel Robinson's had a fall,' he told her.

'Oh, no! Come in and tell me all about it.'

He eyed her dressing-gown longingly, and shook his head. 'No, I mustn't. I ought to get back in case the phone rings again. I just thought I'd let you know — she was a bit worried because she had an appointment with you tomorrow to change her dressing, and she won't be able to come out.'

'I could pop round,' she offered. 'It's right next door.'

Gideon pursed his lips and frowned. 'Community nurses might not like it — poaching from their territory.'

'I guess that depends,' she said philosophically, 'on how busy they are.'

He laughed. 'You're probably right. Ask them. I know she'd rather have you, but they'll be going in anyway to help her wash in the mornings, and put her to bed at night.'

'What's she done?'

He leant against the wall and sighed. 'Nothing much. Bumps and bruises, but I want to keep a close eye on her for thrombosis if she's going to be immobilised for a while. Her venous return is pretty lousy. Still,' he said with a grin, 'she'll soon get bored with sitting in a chair and want to get out and about again, I'm sure. She's too much of a gossip to stay at home. She might miss something.'

Beth laughed. 'You're mean.'

'I am not. She's a terror. Anyway, she sends you her love — said she knew I'd be seeing you tonight.'

Beth's laughter turned to a splutter of horrified astonishment. 'What?'

'You heard. Anyway, I'd better go if we're not to set the tongues wagging. I'll see you tomorrow.'

'Don't I get a kiss?' she said softly.

He groaned, pushed the door shut against prying eyes and took her hungrily into his arms.

'Damn, I want you,' he murmured.

'You could always sneak out after the kids are in bed,' she said wickedly.

He snorted. 'Oh, yeah. I'd be caught.'

She eased out of his arms and slouched provocatively against the wall. 'Not necessarily,' she murmured.

'Witch,' he said softly, and hooking her against him, he kissed her senseless. 'I'll see you tomorrow.'

She watched him go, then closed the door and leant back against it with a satisfied sigh. He's certainly not fighting very hard now, she thought contentedly. Who knows? Given time. . .

* * *

In the morning Beth spoke to the community nurse who was assigned to their practice, and asked if she minded if Beth continued to treat Mrs Robinson's leg ulcer.

'Mind?' she exclaimed. 'My dear, I should be delighted — you wouldn't like to get her up and bath her and do the dressings on her cuts and scrapes, would you?

Beth laughed. 'Sorry, I don't have time. But I'll willingly do her leg. I rather like her.'

The other nurse snorted. 'She's nuts — sticking her nose into everybody's business. It's all right if you've got nothing to hide!'

Beth, who had, blushed slightly but the other woman didn't notice. She was too busy stocking up her bag with supplies, and Beth left her to it, glad to return to her surgery and make a start.

It was almost twelve before she got a chance to go round to Mrs Robinson, and she tapped on the door and went in, calling to her as she did so.

'Hello, dear,' Mrs Robinson called back in her wavering voice. 'In the back room, love. Come on in, Betty'll get you a cup of tea.'

'Oh, how lovely — thank you,' Beth said fervently. It had been one of those hectic and awful mornings, and she was more than ready for a break.

'So, how did you manage to do this?' she asked Mrs Robinson.

'Oh, dear, it was so silly — I went out in the dark because I thought I heard a cat fight and I didn't want my Minnie getting in a nasty scrap when the kittens are still so small — anyway, I'd moved one of my pots to bring in, only it was too heavy for me to lift it over the step and of course — bang! Over it I went!'

'Oh, my goodness! You were lucky not to break something!'

'Don't I know! My friend Audrey went over last winter, and she died of it! Broken hip, she had, and she never did come out of hospital. I lay there and I thought, that's the end for you, my girl. Teach you to gossip so much — that's what I thought!'

'Nonsense, dear,' Betty called from the kitchen. 'Without you life wouldn't be nearly so much fun, would it, Beth?'

'Absolutely not,' Beth said warmly, and patted Mrs Robinson's gnarled old hand.

She turned it over and took Beth's hand, drawing her closer. 'Betty's worse than me,' she whispered, and gave a wheezy laugh.

Betty Maston was the vicar's wife, and Beth had a nodding acquaintance with her due to their proximity in the Close. She had never really spoken to her, though, and was quite surprised when she brought the cup of tea back and set it down beside Beth, perching opposite and laying a hand on her knee.

'I can't tell you what a relief it is that you and Dr Pendragon are going to get married,' she confided. 'That poor man — the things he's had to go through. It's high time he found a good woman to share his life with.'

Beth's jaw must have dropped, because Mrs Maston clapped a hand over her mouth and widened her kindly eyes. 'Oh, I'm sorry, I just assumed — is it still a secret, then?'

'Well —' Beth stalled for time ' — I wouldn't like you to think — there's nothing final.'

'No, well, I expect it won't be long before you set the date,' she said contentedly. 'Of course, you young people do things faster than we used to — I can remember Jeremy courting me all summer before he even kissed me, but he was at theological college — I suppose that might make a difference. But anyway, dear, I'm really pleased for you.'

Beth debated telling her she had complelty the wrong end of the stick, and decided saying nothing was probably the lesser of two evils!

She sipped her tea, then while it cooled she removed the soiled dressing and washed the ulcer with saline.

'Do you know, I think it's improving!' Beth said in surprise.

'Well, I felt it was, but I thought it must be wishful thinking,' Mrs Robinson murmured. 'Well, look at that! It doesn't look so deep — and I reckon it's smaller.'

'Yes, quite a bit — we can dispense with the paste now, I think,' Beth said confidently. 'Well done.'

She finished the dressing, and when she had drunk her cup of tea she excused herself and escaped back to the surgery.

'How's Mabel?' Gideon asked.

She debated telling him about Mrs Maston, and decided not to bother. He would only feel pressured, and no one would dare to repeat it to him, she was sure.

'Better,' she replied instead. 'She's feeling glad to be alive following her fall.'

'Yes, her friend had a fall this time last year and didn't make it. Sad.'

'She told me.'

'Poor old dear. They were very close.'

Beth eyed him. 'You like her too, don't you?'

He grinned. 'Me? Surely not.' He leaned closer and lowered his voice. 'Are you busy tonight?'

She raised one eyebrow a fraction. 'Busy? No.'

'I have to play chess with Michael Roberts, but I thought later. . .'

She let a little smile sneak out. 'Did you?'

'Don't tease,' he growled softly. 'Having an affair with you in this village is going to kill me. It's impossible to keep a secret.'

You're telling me! she thought, but said nothing. What was the point?

'I'll be in,' she told him.

'Good.' He winked. 'I'll see you later — about ten-thirty, eleven?'

Out of the corner of her eye she saw one of Mrs Robinson's cronies heading towards them.

'That'll be fine, Dr Pendragon. I'll put a hot mustard poultice on it.'

His eyes widened in horror, and Beth nearly laughed. 'Hello, Mrs Cripps,' she called sweetly, and Gideon smiled weakly.

'For a moment there. . .' he murmured.

Beth chuckled. 'Gotcha!' she said under her breath, and escaped just before he threw caution to the wind and kissed her right there in the corridor.

He did come round that night — but not in the way Beth had anticipated.

'I want a word,' he said tightly, and she let him in and stood back, bemused.

'Mr Maston — the vicar — told me when I was on my way out to Michael's that he would be delighted to discuss the wedding once we'd decided on the date.' His eyes burned into hers. 'I said I thought he must have the wrong end of the stick, and he said he realised we were still keeping it from the rest of the village, but that you had told his wife this morning at Mabel Robinson's that we were finalising details.'

He paused, clearly waiting for Beth to say something.

She cleared her throat awkwardly.

'Well? Do you deny it?'

She sighed. 'Gideon, it wasn't like that. Obviously she's been watching us, and putting two and two together to make five ——'

'Sounds more like twenty-five to me,' he snapped.

'Oh, come on! She said she was pleased you were getting married at last, and I said — oh I can't remember exactly what I did say — that nothing was final, I think, so she'd leave it alone, but of course she didn't.'

'So why didn't you deny it?'

'Because it would have looked implausible, and I thought it would be better all round to protect our reputations and let her think it was more serious than it is ——'

'So you encouraged her?'

'No, I did not!' Beth said hotly. 'I simply didn't try and deny it, because the next thing was she'd be lecturing me on the nocturnal habits of nice young women and frankly I wasn't in the mood!'

'Oh, weren't you?'

'No, I wasn't — and if you cared a shred for my reputation, you wouldn't expect me to deny it either!'

'Oh, for God's sake! We're both consenting adults — there's no question of protecting our reputations. I'm much more worried about when it gets back to the children,' he said shortly. 'What are you going to come up with then?'

She closed her eyes. 'God knows.'

He sighed heavily. 'This is absolutely typical. This town is so bloody incestuous, you can't even go to the loo without the town crier getting on the phone and telling someone! Well, I'd better get out before someone hears us shouting and starts planning our divorce,' he said bitterly, and turned to the door.

Beth stopped him, just as he was leaving.

'Gideon, I'm sorry, but it wasn't my fault. All right, maybe I should have just denied it, but — well, I didn't. I did what seemed like the right thing at the time, and obviously she took my lack of enthusiasm for a coy attempt at secrecy.'

'So what do I tell the children?' he demanded.

'Nothing.'

'But then they'll hear it on the grapevine ——'

'And you can explain. I wouldn't worry until then.'

He snorted. 'You underestimate the speed of gossip in this town. If I don't wake them up tonight, by tomorrow morning they'll be planning the big day!'

She swallowed. 'Would you like me to talk to them about it? After all, I was there.'

He sighed. 'No, leave it. It's quite possible that they'll hear nothing, and if they don't we'll be saved the embarrassment of explaining just what exactly might have given them the wrong idea.'

He opened the door and stepped out, to be greeted by the vicar's cheerful hail.

'Lovely evening!'

Beth closed her eyes. She was in her dressing-gown, clearly outlined by the light in the hall, and Gideon was just leaving at something before midnight.

Great. So much for damage limitation.

* * *

The children, predictably, did hear about it, and came rushing home from the shops full of excitement.

'Why didn't you tell us?' they demanded.

'Because it isn't true,' Gideon told them flatly. 'We aren't getting married, no matter how badly you and Mrs Robinson and the vicar might want us to, so you can all forget it. I'm going to put a notice up in the Post Office,' he added, and stalked out, banging the door behind him.

It was the outside of enough. Two of his patients had said something to him this morning, and his denials, like Beth's, had been treated indulgently, as much as to say, 'We'll let you have your little secrets, if you must!'. Gideon was furious, all the more angry because there was nothing he could really do about it.

And the look on the children's faces when he'd told them it wasn't true — were they really so keen? he wondered. He supposed they might be, but he really couldn't cope——

He felt panic rising up like bile inside him. Going back into the house, he changed into his running gear and found his son.

'William? You're in charge. Here's ten pounds. I'll see you later.'

He let himself out and set off over the fields. He would run till he was exhausted, and then perhaps he would outrun the fear.

It wasn't Beth — rather the responsibility for another mouth, another psyche, another drain on emotions already stretched to breaking point.

Soon she'd be gone, and things would get back to normal. He'd be better then, he told himself. As the fields flowed away under the steady pounding of his

feet, so the panic ebbed, leaving emptiness in its
wake. . .

The fuss gradually died down, with Beth and Gideon
both explaining to anyone who mentioned their
'engagement' that it was all a misunderstanding and
Beth was, in fact, just acting as a housekeeper and so
naturally they saw a great deal of each other.

Mrs Robinson, of course, didn't quite believe her but
allowed her to have her secret.

Her ulcer continued to improve, and true to Gideon's
word the prospect of staying at home was too much for
her and she was soon up on her feet and out again. Beth
often saw her making her way slowly round the shops,
pausing every few feet for a little natter with one or
other of her cronies.

And as the fuss died down, so Gideon began to relax
again and unbend towards Beth, which made life both
at home and at work much more bearable.

Annabel Steel came back to have her stitches
removed from her fingers, and said that they had been
very sore. 'It was worth it, though — they've really been
listening to what I have to say for once, and they've
promised not to push me.'

Beth smiled. 'Good, that's marvellous.'

'The trouble is,' Annabel said ruefully, 'I really miss
playing the piano these days! Isn't that silly?'

'No — it's human nature. Can you move them well?'

She wiggled her fingers stiffly. 'Not wonderfully — my
right hand's more important really, but it's still going to
be a long time before it's good enough to use for the
pieces I've been playing.'

Beth eyed her movements consideringly. 'I think you

could probably do with some physiotherapy on them. Let me talk to Dr Pendragon about it, and we'll sort something out for you. After all,' she added with a smile, 'you don't want it to have been too effective, do you?'

Annabel gave a wry little grin. 'Do you think I was very stupid?'

Beth shook her head. 'No, just desperate. We all do silly things when we're desperate.'

She spoke to Gideon later about physiotherapy, and he said he'd make enquiries but he was sure it was a three-month wait.

'Could they afford to go privately?'

'What, with the money they're saving on her piano lessons?' he said with a grin. 'Very likely. She's at the same school as Claire and William, so if they can afford the fees they can probably stretch that bit further. I'll ring the mother and have a chat, because in fact there's a very good physio who practises privately in the village.'

He did so, and Annabel started seeing the woman almost immediately. She came back with Claire after school on the next Monday, and told them that her fingers were much less stiff, and she hoped to be able to play again within a couple of weeks.

Beth was able to give Gideon the good news when she went back for the follow-up session of the Stop Smoking clinic that evening.

'Thank God for that—I've been wondering if I shouldn't have sent her in to the hospital for those sutures.'

'But you did a lovely job,' Beth said instantly, and he gave her one of his rare smiles.

'Thank you,' he murmured. His hand came out and brushed her cheek. 'I've missed you. I don't care any more what they say about us, I want to spend some time with you — how about later?'

Beth blushed slightly. Her periods always started on Monday, usually about mid-afternoon. So far this one hadn't, but she knew it would. Since she started taking the Pill she was as regular as clockwork. 'Um — it's not the best time of the month at the moment,' she told him with a shy grin. 'Try later in the week.'

His answering smile was wry. 'We don't have to make love, Beth — although I can't deny I want to. Why don't you stay for a while after supper — have a drink and watch the telly with me.'

'Annabel's there.'

'So? It's all going to be quite respectable, you tell me.'

She laughed. 'OK. Right, where are they all?'

'Maybe they've all lapsed,' he said with a doleful face. 'Perhaps it'll be our worst percentage success rate yet.'

'In which case we can blame it on the floods and the wind,' Beth said breezily. 'It couldn't possibly be our fault.'

He snorted, but then the door opened and Jan and David came in, followed by Paul looking disgustingly pleased with himself.

'No need to ask how it's going,' Gideon said with a laugh.

'Said I'd do it, didn't I?'

'No, *I* said you'd do it,' Gideon corrected him. 'You just did the difficult bit.'

He grinned. 'Whatever — I got there, and Jill's over the moon. Says it's worth washing the curtains now, because they'll stay clean more'n five minutes!'

Everybody laughed, but there were murmurs of agreement, too.

'I washed down the paintwork — you should have seen the difference!' Jan Driscoll said. 'Makes you wonder what you did to your lungs.'

They shared notes, bolstered each other's spirits, and realised that everyone else, too, was still finding it difficult occasionally.

'I can't go down the pub at all,' Paul said dolefully.

'Should think Jill's pleased about that, too,' one of the other women said.

'I find if I pass someone in the street — especially if they've just lit up — that's the killer for me. I want to follow them, sniffing their smoke!' David Hendry told them. 'It can be very embarrassing!'

They all chuckled.

'How about a go on the smokerlyser?' Beth suggested. 'It's not very long for some of you, but you may find a significant decrease in your blood carbon monoxide levels, even so. Want to try?'

They were all enthusiastic, and Beth recorded all the results and noted the improvement.

David Hendry's was the biggest, although as the heaviest smoker initially and the most consistently reformed of the group, that was to be expected.

Paul Stone's fall in level was only slight, but nevertheless it was there, and he was able to see that given time he would improve.

All in all, it was a very encouraging follow-up session, and they all went away feeling very proud of themselves and determined to carry on the good work.

'Ninety-per-cent success rate, so far,' Beth said.

Gideon grinned. 'I reckon it's actually a hundred per

cent, because the woman who dropped out right at the start was clearly not motivated. She only came because her husband told her to, and without a personal reason it's impossible. So, yes, I reckon we can call it a hundred per cent. And that,' he added, 'needs celebrating. Come on, shove this lot back in the cupboard and let's go.'

'What about the cups?'

'Dump them in the sink — Mrs Horrell can deal with them in the morning.'

They went back, full of high spirits, and after a lovely rich casserole and some extremely wicked apple pie, they settled down in front of the television. Gideon propped his feet on the coffee table, Beth snuggled up beside him under his arm, and they channel-hopped and chatted over a couple of glasses of smooth, old port.

At about eight-thirty Annabel and Claire came in to say they were going to bed, and Annabel's eyebrows shot up.

As they left the room Beth could hear Claire saying, 'Don't mind them, they carry on all the time when no one's looking. Everyone in the village reckons they're getting married soon. It's dead romantic.'

Beside her, Beth could feel Gideon stiffen. She reached up her hand and smoothed his jaw, feeling the roughness of stubble under her fingertips, and beneath the skin his jaw clenched.

'It's all right,' she soothed. 'Just kids talking the way they do.'

He snorted. 'Did you hear her? Dead romantic, indeed!'

Beth sighed. It was, in fact, quite romantic sitting cuddled up together sharing their day, sipping port and enjoying the odd companionable silence. Until his remark she had allowed herself to enjoy it. Now she realised she had probably enjoyed it too much, and certainly more than Gideon.

She straightened away from him. 'I'd better go—we don't want the girls to get the wrong idea.'

'Beth, I didn't mean——'

He broke off, and she turned and met his eyes levelly. 'What didn't you mean, Gideon?'

He looked away. 'Oh, hell—you're right, you'd better go. I'll see you in the morning.'

She stood up, leant over and kissed him lightly on the lips, pressing him back into the settee. 'You stay there, I'll let myself out.'

She went home, washed and climbed into her lonely bed, and wondered if he would ever allow himself to love her—or if he did, if he would ever allow that love to run its course.

As time wore on, so she began to think her earlier optimism, though slight, had been misplaced.

They found the odd occasion when they could be alone together, but she no longer told him that she loved him. His reluctance to accept her feelings and his guilt over his treatment of her made them both uncomfortable. It was easier if she didn't say the words aloud.

Instead she showed him, with her lips and hands and body, bringing all her soul to their lovemaking.

And Gideon, although he didn't realise it, did the same. He couldn't have touched her as he did, held her as he did, cried out for her as he did, if there was no love in his heart.

It didn't, though, alter his resolve, and that was the part she found so hard to bear.

They were both busy at work. There was a flu epidemic, and on the nights when he was on call she heard his car go out several times a night.

The surgery was awash with people suffering secondary infections following their flu — ear infections, sinusitis, persistent sore throats — the symptoms were as many as the patients, and all the staff were exhausted.

The inoculation programme was stepped up, and Beth was kept busier than usual.

On top of that, Christmas was fast approaching. She made an angel's constume for Sophie, and helped at the school with the preparations for the nativity play. They were still in their makeshift quarters while the school was repaired, and Beth found the noise and clamour of all the little people strangely soothing. They were all so well, so happy, so vibrant!

And Sophie, more than any other, played on her heartstrings.

If she had been Gideon's child, she could have understood her feelings, but she wasn't. Yet still Beth loved her desperately, and knew that parting from her in the spring would be the hardest thing she had ever done.

No, leaving Gideon would be the hardest thing, but in a way that would be easier because it was his stubbornness that would lead to their parting.

Leaving Sophie, on the other hand, would hurt them both, and Sophie was completely innocent. That was the difference.

One Friday evening at the end of November, Gideon

came home after surgery looking flushed, his eyes over-bright, his skin hot and dry.

'Bed,' she said firmly, and he went without protest.

William came in just as she was pushing a naked and shivering Gideon under the bedclothes.

'What's going on?'

'Your father's got flu — go on, out, you don't want it. Go and put the kettle on.'

She made him a drink of honey and lemon, laced with aspirin, and he sipped it half-heartedly and then flung back the bedclothes and stumbled into the bathroom. She heard retching, and then gargling, and after a few minutes he reappeared.

'God, I feel lousy,' he croaked.

'Come on, back to bed. I'll sponge you down.'

'What's my temperature?'

'God knows — sky-high, I expect. Get into bed, I'll take it. Where's the thermometer?'

'In my bag — in the hall.'

He slumped into bed and dragged the quilt up, coughing harshly.

With a soft sigh Beth left the room and ran down to the hall. Gideon's bag was there and she took it back up.

'What's the combination?'

'Phone number,' he mumbled.

She fiddled with the combination lock, and eventually she managed to open it and find the thermometer. She slipped it under his tongue and took the opportunity to check his other observations.

His pulse was racing, over a hundred, and she could feel from the temperature of his skin that he was way over normal. His respiration rate was almost doubled, and as she watched him a shudder ran over him.

She removed the thermometer from his mouth and stared at it in disbelief.

'What is it?' he croaked.

'Forty point one — over a hundred and four.'

Ruthlessly she yanked off the bedclothes, covering him instead with a warm sheet from the airing cupboard, and then she started sponging him down with warm water.

'I'm freezing,' he said through clenched teeth.

'I wish you were. Come on, you know I have to do this.'

She swept the warm flannel down the inside of his arm and over his fingers, then back up the outside, repeating it on the other arm, then she did the same for his legs.

'You're thinner,' she observed. 'You've been working too hard and not eating regularly.'

'Don't talk about eating,' he mumbled, and a shiver ran over him.

She kept on, bathing and soothing, talking softly to him as she washed him again and again, and gradually his shivers died away and his eyes drifted shut.

She took his temperature again and saw it was down to thirty-nine point six, just over a hundred and three. Better, but not much.

She went and made him another drink, and when she brought it up he was shivering again.

It was a long night, and the day that followed was no better. William insisted on helping and took turns sponging him down, and by Sunday afternoon he was beginning to look more human.

Beth, however, was exhausted and went home to bed, leaving Gideon in Will's care.

She woke in the night shivering, and laid her hand on her abdomen. Burning. Oh, God.

Shivering violently, she forced herself out of bed and went into the bathroom, sitting on the side of the bath and wiping her arms and legs with a wet flannel.

It was horrible, and after a while she was sick. Once she'd started, she didn't seem to be able to stop.

She was freezing, sitting on the floor in the bathroom in just a flimsy nightie, with the heating long since gone off and a temperature that she knew was up in the gods. She ought to get back to bed, but somehow she couldn't find the strength. . .

Hot, heavy tears rolled down her cheeks, and she turned her face to the wall and cried like a baby.

He felt better—still weak, but his temperature was back to normal and with any luck he would be able to go back to work tomorrow. He didn't want to let his colleagues down; they had enough to do.

He went down to the kitchen and put the kettle on to make himself a cup of tea, and as he did so he glanced out of the window.

Odd. Beth's bathroom light was on, and it wasn't normally. Perhaps she'd forgotten to turn it off—or maybe she just needed the loo. Damn, she was entitled.

He made the tea and went back up to his room, and on the way he checked Sophie. She was fine, cool and peaceful, and he glanced out of her window.

The light was still on.

He shrugged. So what. He could hardly go over there and wake her up just to tell her she'd left the light on.

But what if she was ill? She had no way of calling for help.

He put his tea down, pulled on some clothes and let himself quietly out of the house.

As he opened her door, he could hear the muffled sound of her crying, and his heart wrenched.

He ran up the stairs and across the room to the bathroom, and found her hunched up in the corner, her slender shoulders racked with harsh, dry sobs.

She felt as if she was on fire, and he gathered her into his arms and lifted her carefully, carrying her back to bed.

'It's all right, sweetheart — I'm here, I'll take care of you. You lie there, I'll sponge you down and you'll soon feel better.'

Her eyes flickered open and she gazed at him. 'Gideon?' she whispered 'Oh, I prayed you'd come — I feel so ill. . .'

'Shhh. . .' He smoothed her hair back from her burning face and dropped a kiss on her cheek. 'It's all right now. You just lie there and be a good girl.'

He filled the washing-up bowl and took it over to her bedside table, then found the flannel on the bathroom floor where she had dropped it.

Like him, she protested and tried to wriggle back under the bedclothes, but slowly, steadily, he worked on her until her temperature was down to reasonable proportions.

He found some soluble aspirin and made her take it, then, exhausted and shaking himself, he pulled off his clothes and crawled into bed beside her.

'Gideon?' she murmured sleepily.

'Go to sleep — I'm here.'

'Thanks,' she mumbled, and then she drifted off to sleep.

He lay beside her, careful not to touch her in case he made her hot, but when he woke later she was draped across him like a sheet, still burning hot but apparently unable to stay away.

He eased out from under her and filled the bowl with warm water again.

'No,' she protested sleepily, and she wriggled away from him.

He followed her, sponging and soothing, and finally her temperature dropped again and she slept peacefully.

Gideon, exhausted and not nearly as well as he had thought, sprawled on the little sofa and fell asleep.

That was how William found them at something after seven. He woke his father, told him he would drop Sophie at a friend's house so her mother could take her to school, and said he'd done the lunches. 'I saw the lights on and realised what had happened,' he explained, and with the small part of his brain that was still able to function Gideon was grateful that he hadn't crawled back into bed with Beth.

That would have taken some living down!

CHAPTER NINE

BETH's flu left her feeling weak and exhausted. Gideon stayed with her for the whole of that day, and he made her take the rest of the week off.

'Including the house,' he told her firmly.

'But how will you cope?' she asked

'We'll cope. You just get better.'

Considering how pale and tired he looked, she wondered how on earth they would manage. However, he would brook no argument, and frankly, she was grateful, because she felt sick and absolutely wiped out.

It was Saturday before it occurred to her that she had missed a period that week. Still, they weren't true periods, only withdrawal bleeding on the Pill, so perhaps the flu had messed her system up. She started on the next course on the correct day and decided she was being melodramatic. She couldn't possibly be pregnant, she had taken her pills on time faithfully. The only time she had been a little late with them was during the week of the flood and the storm, and then she had lapsed twice, but she had had a period since then, so she couldn't be pregnant.

No, it must be the flu.

She went back to work on Monday, still tired and a litte nauseated but feeling much stronger. It was the second week in December, and Christmas was coming up all too fast.

After Christmas was the New Year, and in March

Stephanie would be back, assuming everything went well with the baby which was due at the beginning of January — and then Beth would be gone.

Fortunately she was too busy to dwell on it, because work was as frantic as ever. Molly had been off with flu too, and the temp they had got from the agency had been useless. Consequently when Molly returned she had the mammoth task of setting things to rights again, and her temper suffered as a result.

Beth didn't feel well enough to offer to help, so kept out of the way, which ironically was probably the most helpful thing she could have done.

Brian Hurley came to see her, his thumb still not properly healed from the accident back in mid-October.

She called Gideon on the phone. 'Mr Hurley's here — I think he's got a persistent sinus in this thumb. Do you want to see him?'

'Mmm — yes please. Keep him there, I'll be with you in a tick.'

He arrived a minute later and nodded thoughtfully. 'Yes, I think you're right. Well, Mr Hurley, what do you want to do? I could open it up for you and see if we can find the bit of wood that's obviously left in there, or we could just leave it and wait for it to work its way up.'

The man frowned at his hand. 'Well, I don't rightly know, Doc — what would you advise?'

'I think I'd like to open it up — just to get things moving a little quicker. I imagine you'd like to get back to work as quickly as possible?'

'Well, I would, and of course while it's like this I can't — I work in the food industry and we're not allowed to work with any infected areas on our hands.'

'Right. Let's book you in, then — how about later

today? Sister Turner, could you manage that? I know Sister Rudd's too busy, but I could fit it in at two, if you could assist?'

'Of course. It won't take too long, will it?'

He shook his head. 'No — half an hour at the most. Is that all right, Mr Hurley?'

The man nodded, and Beth redressed the thumb and sent him on his way.

Mrs Robinson was next, her leg ulcer almost completely healed.

'I think you'll be right as rain for Christmas,' Beth told her.

'Oh, what a relief! It's been such a long old job.'

'Yes, these ulcers can be. Still, things are looking up now. How are the kittens?'

'Oh, growing apace. I don't suppose you know anybody who could take one, could you? I thought I'd found homes for them all, but Winnie said she'd have two and she's been so poorly she didn't think it was right, just in case — you know, so I wondered if you could think of anyone? Perhaps when you do your surgeries, if you could ask around? They'll be ready to go in the New Year.'

Beth promised to do so, and then after her surgery finished she went home and made a start on the washing before going back to the surgery for Mr Hurley's operation.

While she was sorting out the clothes on the floor in the utility-room, a mouse ran across in front of her. She shrieked and shot backwards, hand over her heart, and then stood there laughing helplessly and telling herself not to be so absurd.

'It's probably much more frightened than you are,'

she said in a voice designed to bolster her confidence, and cautiously, one eye on the corner the mouse had run into, she finished sorting the clothes, loaded the washing machine and set it going.

Back at the surgery she mentioned the mouse to Gideon.

'Oh, not again. We used to have a cat years ago and it kept them down quite nicely, but since it died we've had the odd one or two—I expect with the cold they've all come inside.'

An idea occurred to Beth. 'Um—Mrs Robinson's got two kittens she needs to find homes for.'

'Oh, no—no, Beth, absolutely not! I've got enough to worry about without having kittens getting lost and ripping up the carpets and clawing the furniture. I've been down that road, and frankly, you can forget it. Believe me, by comparison the mice are no trouble at all.'

'They aren't very sanitary.'

'Nor are cats,' he retorted. 'Did you ever know a cat that would stay off the worktops? You can't leave anything out.'

'But you don't. Anyway,' she added, mercilessly going for his Achilles' heel, 'the children would love it. Children ought to have pets, it's good for them. Teaches care and consideration for other species, and with the world in the state it's in that can't be a bad thing.'

He lounged back against his desk and crooked an eyebrow at her. 'Is that a fact?'

She struggled against the smile. 'You know it's true.'

'Hmm. Is Mr Hurley here yet?'

'Yes—I'll get him.'

She went out and called him, and while Gideon was

getting scrubbed and gowned ready, she helped Mr Hurley out of his coat and on to the couch in the treatment room they used for minor surgical procedures.

She supported his arm on an extension and draped it with sterile cloths, then Gideon swabbed it down and infiltrated the area with lignocaine.

After a few minutes it was completely numb, and she handed Gideon a scalpel and watched as he carefully opened the wound.

She swabbed the exudate, and Gideon used the electrocauteriser to stop the bleeding in the tiny vessels.

'Right, I can see the hole — now, where's that splinter — aha!' Using the tweezers, he freed a nasty piece of rotten wood and lifted it up for Mr Hurley to see. 'Got it!'

'Well, I'll be — fancy that great thing being in there and not hurting!'

'Well, it's quite soft now, of course, but it was preventing you from healing. It'll race away now.'

He cleaned the wound, excised the necrosed tissue and dusted it with antibiotic, then closed it carefully. Beth put a dressing on it and Gideon advised him to come back in a week to have the stitches out. 'Come back sooner if you're worried, though,' he added.

As the man went out, Gideon glanced up at the clock on the wall. 'Twenty-nine minutes,' he told Beth. 'Not a bad guess.'

She grinned at him. 'What's it like to be wonderful?'

His eyes softened. 'You tell me.'

With a single stride he crossed the room and pushed the door to, then pulled her into his arms. 'God, I need you,' he murmured. 'It's been so long.'

'Only just over a week,' she protested.

'Nearly two. Are you home tonight?'

'You know I am.'

'I'll come over later.'

She smiled seductively. 'I'll be waiting.'

'Don't do that,' he grated. 'There's a couch over there behind you——'

'Yes. It looks very comfortable.'

'So don't tempt me.'

She grinned. 'Spoilsport. I'll see you later.'

'You bet.'

She went home and put the washing in the tumble drier, then went back into the kitchen. She had set some vegetables out on the worktop to prepare later for supper, and she looked at them in horror. There were tiny teethmarks in the carrots, and a little trail of droppings.

Sweeping the vegetables into the bin, she washed down the surfaces in bleach and started again. She would have to tell him about it later—but much later, when they were on their own and she could push him a little about the cats. If she said anything in front of the children it would only upset them if he still refused, and she knew from bitter experience how stubborn he could be once he made his mind up.

In fact, when the time came she didn't have to talk him into it at all—he was much more concerned about something else. . .

It was nearly midnight, and the house was finally quiet. Gideon switched off the television and went through to the kitchen, his mind on Beth. The kids had taken ages to settle, and his frustration was mounting by the second. God, he needed her. It seemed like months since he'd felt her warm, supple body beneath his——

'Hi, Dad.'

He jumped guiltily, his hand on the back door knob. 'Um—William! I thought you'd gone to bed.'

He shook his head 'Nah—couldn't sleep. I came down to make a drink. Where are you going?'

Gideon's mind emptied. 'Um—for a walk—clear my head.'

'In this?'

He opened the back door and stared blankly out into the pouring rain.

'Oh.' He shut the door again. 'Perhaps I won't bother.'

William gave him an awkward grin. 'Dad, why don't you just go to her?'

He felt the dull flush crawl up his neck and over his cheekbones. 'What do you mean?' he said, clawing for time.

'Beth,' Will said patiently. 'Look, it's OK, you know. You're both consenting adults—why not?'

Gideon's only thought was for denial. This was his son, telling him it was all right to have a sex life! He was completely fazed.

'Uh—whatever gives you the idea——?'

William rolled his eyes. 'Oh, Dad! Give me a little credit. Anyway,' he continued, 'when you were ill last week—well, you said all sorts of things.'

Gideon swallowed. 'What sorts of things?' he asked weakly.

'Oh—well. . .' It was William's turn to blush. 'I won't repeat them, but—well, there were times when you must have thought I was Beth——'

Gideon groaned. This was awful.

'— and another time, when you knew it was me, you were telling me — oh, hell, it doesn't matter.'

Gideon thought it probably did matter, very much, but he hardly dared to ask. He had to, though.

'What was I telling you?'

'Oh — father-and-son sort of stuff — about finding myself a girl like that and treating her right. Making sure I didn't get her pregnant. You told me. . .'

'What? What did I tell you?'

'Well, that it was OK for you and Beth because she was on the Pill, but that — '

'I told you that?'

William nodded, clearly embarrassed.

He was nothing like as embarrassed as his father. 'Ah, look, um — ' He cleared his throat and tried again. 'This conversation — '

'Don't worry, Dad, I won't tell anyone.'

'I wouldn't want Claire to know.'

William laughed. 'She keeps telling me she thinks you're sleeping together.'

He blinked. 'She does?'

Will sighed. 'Dad, we're older than you think. I'll be eighteen just after Christmas — legally adult, and since her periods have started Claire's grown up enormously. Believe me, if you want to have an affair with someone, we can cope.'

Gideon stabbed his fingers through his hair, stunned by his son's casual acceptance of something he was still struggling with himself. 'I'm not going to marry her,' he said finally. 'So don't hold your breath. This *is* just an affair.'

'She loves you.'

His jaw clenched. 'I know.'

'And you love her too.'

'I do not.'

'Yes you do. Why won't you admit it and marry her? Dad, all women can't be like Mum.'

His eyes shot up and locked with his son's, so like his in every way.

'Don't you believe it,' he said softly. 'We're better off without any added complications.'

'She's not a complication, Dad,' William said gently. 'She's a woman — a warm, lovely woman, and she thinks the world of you.'

Gideon swallowed the sudden lump in his throat. If only Beth had been William's mother, how different his life would have been.

'Don't hurt her, Dad,' Will pleaded softly. 'Please, don't hurt her.'

Gideon sighed. 'I didn't want to, Will, but I'm afraid I already have.'

'Dad?' William said after a moment.

'Mmm?'

'There's a mouse on the worktop.'

'What!'

He spun round just in time to see the mouse shoot round behind the breadbin.

'We need a cat,' Will said calmly. 'Mrs Robinson's got two kittens going begging.'

Gideon narrowed his eyes at his son. 'Did Beth tell you that?'

'No — Mrs R. did, in the shop. Asked if I knew anybody who wanted one. I said I'd ask around.'

Gideon opened the breadbin and saw two startled little eyes peering at him, before the mouse threw itself out over the top of the worktop and fled under a cupboard.

'Damn it! They're everywhere!'

'So can we have a cat?'

Gideon threw the bread in the bin on top of Beth's carrots, and sighed. 'I reckon we'll have to.'

Will laughed. 'Great — Sophie will be tickled to death, and so will Beth — she loves cats.'

'Humph.'

'Humph nothing. I'm going to bed. Go and see her, Dad. Maybe sex will improve your temper.'

He got out of the kitchen in the nick of time.

'I thought you were never coming,' Beth said softly.

Gideon shot her a rueful grin and yanked off his jumper. 'Will caught me on the way out — I'm here with his blessing.'

'What?'

He gave a short laugh. 'Yes. He thinks sex might improve my temper — oh, and we do need a cat,' he added as he sat on the edge of the bed and pulled off his shoes. 'The kitchen is hopping with mice.'

Beth watched hungrily as he slid down the zip and pushed his trousers down over his hips.

'Come here,' she murmured huskily. 'I want to hold you.'

He joined her under the quilt, taking her in his arms and locking their mouths together in a deep lingering kiss.

'Oh, Beth, I needed that,' he murmured as he came up for air.

'Has Will been giving you a hard time?'

'Mmm,' he mumbled, his mouth closing hotly over a

rosy nipple. She shuddered slightly, her fingers thread-ing through his hair, cradling his head against her breasts. They were tender and aching, yearning for his touch, and they were generously rewarded.

Still, somehow, it wasn't enough. His hand slid down to her waist, over the slight flare of her hip and round, teasing the damp tangle of curls.

Her breath caught in her throat, and she arched up against his palm, aching for him. Her hand reached down, cupping his heavy fullness, drawing a deep groan from his lips.

Nudging her thighs apart he settled between them, then cupping her bottom in his hands he slid deeply into her with a shuddering sigh. 'Beth,' he rasped, and then his mouth found hers again and there were no more words, just the whispered symphony of their loving to break the silence of the night.

'So when are you going to get the cat?' she asked later, as they lay in a sated tangle of arms and legs.

'Oh, I have no idea. I'm beginning to wonder if it isn't really rather stupid.'

'Oh, no I think it's a wonderful idea.' She was silent for a moment, her fingers tracing the soft curls on his chest. 'Of course two cats would keep each other company. . .'

'No.'

Her fingers inched lower. 'Oh, go on. They're brother and sister—they'd have such fun together.'

'Yeah—making incestuous babies. No.'

'Oh, you'd have to have them done.'

'Two lots of vet bills. No—ah, love, stop!'

Her hand stilled. 'Really?'

He shot her a crooked grin. 'No, not really. You carry on, it's wonderful.'

'Two cats?'

'No.'

She withdrew her hand.

'Tease,' he shot at her.

'Mm-hm.'

He laughed, soft and low and husky, and reached for her. 'We'll see about that.'

With one swift move he covered her, his body sinking deeply into hers.

The cats were forgotten.

Christmas was coming up with horrifying rapidity. Beth took the children Christmas shopping for Gideon's presents, and they asked her what she was getting him.

'I don't know — any ideas?'

'There's a music box in the antique shop in the square,' Will told her. 'He keeps looking at it, but he won't buy it.'

'Why not?' she asked, thinking that it was probably prohibitively expensive.

'I don't know — he was very odd about it. Do you want to go round now? I'll show you.'

They left Claire with Sophie and went round to the shop. It was in the window, and Will pointed it out to her.

'There — that little wooden box with the inlaid top.'

Beth asked to look at it, and was pleased to discover it was only slightly over her budget. Not that it would have made any difference, she decided, because Gideon liked it. She turned it over in her hands and wound it, and then opened the lid. It had a very pretty inlay and the notes were pure and true. 'It's the Brahms' Cradle Song,' Beth said softly.

'It's for a nursery, really,' the woman who was serving her said. 'Well, most of them were. It's cheaper than it ought to be, because it's been slightly damaged from being in the damp at some time — see, here, the veneer on the back has lifted a bit but it could always be repaired.'

'I'll take it — and if Dr Pendragon comes in to look at it again, could you tell him someone from London bought it? It won't be a lie, because I am from London, but I want it to be a surprise.'

The woman's eyes lit up. 'My pleasure — he'll be delighted with it. He keeps looking at it in the window, but he won't come in after it, I'm sure. If he'd been going to buy it he would have done. He's usually so decisive.'

'Well, he's vacillated too long this time,' Beth said cheerfully. She picked up a little crystal scent bottle with a silver stopper. 'Oh, how pretty.'

'Yes, it is. It's early Victorian.'

Beth looked at the price tag and set it down regretfully. 'I've already overspent. Perhaps another day.'

They left the shop, and she smiled at Will. 'Thank you — that was a brilliant idea.'

He grinned. 'My pleasure. I'm full of them, and I'm always willing to share.'

She laughed, ridiculously pleased with her purchase, and took it back and wrapped it before Gideon could see it lying around in her flat.

That was the Saturday before Claire and Will broke up for the Christmas holidays, and the next day was the Christmas carol service at their school.

'Beth, will you come?' Claire asked.

'Oh — you don't want me there.'

'I'm in the choir — Beth, you have to come! Please! I'll simply *die* if you're not there!'

She was helpless against Claire's pleading. 'May I?' she asked Gideon.

'You don't really want to come, do you?' he asked her.

'Not if you don't think it would be a good idea.'

Claire was frankly puzzled. 'Why wouldn't it be a good idea?'

'Because people talk,' Beth said gently. 'There's enough gossip about us without adding fuel to the fire.'

But Claire was unconvinced. 'How is your coming to the carol service adding fuel to the fire? You don't have to sit with Dad!'

'I'm sure it won't make any difference one way or the other,' Gideon said soothingly. 'If Beth would like to come, then of course she's welcome, and of course she'll sit with me. I just don't want you putting pressure on her.'

'But I wouldn't!'

'Not much.'

Beth laughed. 'It's all right, Gideon. I would like to come, really.'

So it was decided, and she sat with Gideon, Sophie between them, and the carols brought tears to her eyes.

Will read one of the lessons, looking and sounding so much like his father that she got a huge lump in her throat. She felt absurdly proud of him. If only she could have been his mother. . .

It was impossible, of course, she was far too young to have been the mother of any of them except the little scrap snuggled up beside her, her thumb in her mouth, her eyelids drooping. But Sophie, with her blonde hair and blue eyes, could almost have been her own. . .

The following day Mr Hurley came back to have his stitches out, and Beth was delighted to see that the thumb had healed almost completely.

'That's marvellous,' she told him, and he left the surgery thoroughly pleased with himself.

One person slightly less pleased with herself was Annabel Steel, who was still finding difficulty with her piano-playing following her self-inflicted injury.

She was still having regular physiotherapy, but over the years she had reached a standard where the slightest flaw in the performance of her fingers was disastrous. So she was frustrated, and her parents were racked with guilt for pushing her too hard, and it was really a rather sorry scenario all round.

The only good thing to come out of it was the communication that had opened up between them all since the incident, and that, Beth felt sure, was worth more than all the piano-playing expertise in the world. If only *her* mother had listened to her, but Beth had had no sanctions, unlike Annabel. There was nothing Beth could have done to make her own parents sit up and take notice, because there was no area — at least no academic area — in which she shone.

Not, that was, to two Classics scholars.

Gideon had asked her what she was doing for Christmas, and was horrified when she told him that she had no plans.

'What about your family?' he asked.

She shrugged. 'My parents are in Crete, researching

some mythical god. Christmas doesn't compare with that really, does it?'

The hurt must have shown in her voice because he took her in his arms and held her tenderly while he asked her to join them. 'Strictly off-duty, though,' he added. 'I'll do the lunch and you'll just sit back and enjoy yourself — OK?'

She swallowed hard. It was years since she had had a real family Christmas — not since before her grandfather had died and her grandmother had gone into a home had her family made anything of the festival, and she found herself looking forward to it more and more.

Claire and William broke up in the middle of that week, and the infectious excitement of Christmas began to invade the big old house.

Decorations were dragged out of attic cupboards, recipes were pored over and Sophie became desperately over-excited.

Her Nativity play at school was on the Tuesday before Christmas, and Gideon was too busy to take the time off.

'Will you go for me?' he asked Beth. 'She adores you — she'd probably rather have you there than me anyway.'

Did she imagine it or was there a trace of hurt in his voice? Surely not — little Sophie worshipped him.

She went to the Nativity play with William and Claire, and Sophie tripped up the step and started to cry. Then she saw them and a wobbly smile spread over her face, and from then on she was wonderful — if a touch forgetful. She was only one of the 'chorus' angels, so there were plenty of others to keep her in line, but she was distinctly stage-struck and Will was convulsed.

'She's sweet, don't be so mean,' Claire hissed crossly.

'Of course she is — he knows that,' Beth soothed.

They clapped like mad at the end, and after it was over Sophie came tripping out, glitter-spray still in her hair and rouge on her cheeks.

'Did you see me? I was an angel!' she said proudly. 'Did you like me?'

'You were wonderful, pumpkin,' Will said lovingly and scooped her up in his arms for a big hug.

'Beth, did you like me?' she asked worriedly.

'I thought you were wonderful, poppet — the prettiest angel ever!'

'Really?'

'Absolutely!' Beth said solemnly.

'Claire?'

'Super — clever girl.' Sophie leant over Will's arm and Claire gave her a big kiss.

They took her home, and a little later Gideon came back. 'So how was my star?' he asked seriously.

'I fell upstairs, and cried, and I was wonderful — Beth said I was the prettiest angel ever.'

A heart-wrenching little smile brushed his lips and he hugged her. 'I'm sure. Well done, Tuppence,' he said warmly, and Beth's heart ached for him.

Christmas Eve dawned cold and bright. Gideon had a surgery and wasn't off till lunchtime, and by the time he came home all that was left to do was decorating the tree.

He had already bought it and put it in a pot, and he brought it in and stood it in the corner of the drawing room.

They all decorated it together, and then all the presents were placed underneath it.

They went together to midnight mass in the church next door, and Mrs Maston sidled up to Beth afterwards.

'Merry Christmas, dear,' she said, and then, lowering her voice, added, 'Had any thoughts about the date yet?'

Beth smiled and shook her head.

In fact she had been thinking about dates, a lot, but not in the way Mrs Maston meant.

Her dress that she had put on that evening had been tight — not noticeably, but considering it had been loose before. . .

And that business of the last missed period. Beth had been convinced she couldn't be pregnant, because she had had a period before that, but looking back on it it had been shorter than usual, and very light.

She could, in fact, have been pregnant for weeks — almost twelve weeks, in fact.

It was time to tell Gideon.

CHAPTER TEN

'PREGNANT? How can you possibly be pregnant?'

He sounded outraged, and so she replied a little more acidly than she would otherwise have done.

'You tell me — you were there at the time.'

'But you're on the Pill — or you told me you were.'

That stung. She tipped her chin and met his eyes. 'I *am* on the Pill.'

'Then you can't be pregnant. It's not possible.'

'Oh, come on, Gideon, of course it's possible.'

'Only if you take them in handfuls because you're careless. How many periods have you missed?'

'One — nearly four weeks ago.'

'So you aren't quite eight weeks.'

She got a sudden, sickening feeling of *déjà vu*. 'Don't you dare suggest I have an abortion!' she whispered shakily.

He looked shocked. 'I wouldn't. Don't worry, I'll shoulder my responsibilities, Beth.'

She didn't want the baby to be a responsibility — she wanted it to be a joy. As they had walked back from the church she had planned how she would tell him, and foolishly, knowing how he loved his children, she had allowed herself to imagine his delighted response. Unfortunately, knowing also how heavy he found the burden of responsibility for their care, she had ignored the possibility that he might not be pleased to have another child thrust upon him.

173

They had sent the children off to bed, and just when Beth was about to broach the subject Gideon had sat her down in the drawing-room.

'I wanted to give you your present, now, while there was no one else around.' He placed a little gift box in her lap and stood back, looking awkward. 'I hope you like it — I understand you do. It wasn't my first choice, but unfortunately someone else got there first.'

She opened the box with trembling fingers, wondering if she should be doing this before she told him, and found inside the little silver-stoppered scent bottle she had admired in the antique shop in the square.

'Oh, Gideon — thank you! Oh, but you shouldn't, it cost a fortune ——'

He waved that aside. 'Do you like it, really? I was going to get you a music box, but it had gone by the time I made up my mind.'

She laughed softly at the irony, and kneeling down, she pulled his present out from under the tree. She handed it up to him.

'Here — this is for you.'

He tore the paper off and gave a startled laugh. 'But — she said a man from London had bought it.'

'No, someone from London — if she followed my instructions. Will told me you'd been looking at it — I thought you wanted it for yourself.'

His fingers traced the delicate inlay, and his mouth softened. 'I do — it's lovely. Thank you, Beth.'

He pulled her to her feet and kissed her.

'Happy Christmas,' he murmured.

She swallowed. Now was the time.

'Actually, it's rather more appropriate than I had

realised.' She let out a shaky sigh. 'Gideon, I think I'm pregnant.'

She ought to have expected his reaction, she thought now. Responsibility should have been his middle name.

He sat down on the settee and stared into the fire. 'So, when's it due?'

She sat down, also on the settee but at the other end. 'July, I think. About the eleventh.'

She could hear his mind working. 'But — that means you got pregnant in October!'

She nodded. 'I think I must have done. I was late taking it a couple of times — the nights of the flood and the storm — that's the only time I can think of.'

'And that weekend. . .' He let the words trail off. No elaboration was necessary. That weekend they had spent almost entirely in bed, exploring each other with single-minded fascination, entirely dedicated to pleasure.

'It took you long enough to tell me,' he said bitterly after a pause.

'I didn't know. It was only this evening when I put this dress on and it was tight — it always used to fit. Other things have got a bit snug, but I put it down to all the meals I've been eating with you and the children. It never occurred to me. . .'

'You're sure? Perhaps I should look at you.'

The thought of him examining her, his hands that had brought her to such ecstasy touching her so clinically, made her want to weep.

'It isn't necessary,' she said quietly. 'I've been here before, I know the signs. I don't know why I didn't notice them before.'

'Signs?'

'Nausea, tiredness—I thought it was the flu, but it doesn't last this long, and you don't tend to get bigger and lose weight at the same time.'

He sighed and stabbed his fingers through his hair. 'But you must have missed another period, an earlier one.'

She shook her head. 'No. It was lighter, but I still had one, or enough of one to lull me.'

He stood up and paced over to the fire, propping one foot on the fender and staring down into the flames.

'It's a hell of a Christmas present,' he said at last.

'I don't suppose Joseph was exactly ecstatic,' she retorted sharply.

Gideon snorted. 'There was nothing immaculate about this baby's conception,' he said bitterly. 'If I remember rightly——'

'Don't!' she cried, her hands over her ears. 'What we did was beautiful, and I won't listen to you make our baby's conception cheap and torrid!'

He was silent for a moment, his jaw working, then he gave a ragged sigh.

'We'll get married as soon as Mr Maston can fit it in.'

Beth was hurt by this assumption. 'You haven't asked me yet.'

He glared at her. 'I thought this was what you wanted all along!'

'But not like this,' she said sadly.

'Well, I'm sorry, that's the way it is. We're having a baby, and we'll do it properly. Don't worry, Beth, I'll stand by you, and I'll be a good husband and a good father to our baby.'

Her eyes filled and overflowed, and with a sigh he

drew her against his chest and held her gently. 'Don't cry, love, please — don't cry.'

She didn't remember much about Christmas. The children were delighted with the news that they were getting married, but they kept the baby's existence a secret.

Gideon's good cheer was a little forced, but Beth thought she was the only one to notice — perhaps because hers was, too.

He was on call over Boxing Day, and Beth spent the day with the children playing Monopoly and Scrabble and watching television and eating too many chocolates.

She had a desperate craving for them, and by the time Gideon got home after the emergency surgery there were very few left.

'My caramels!' he grumbled.

She gave him a sheepish smile. 'I seem to have had them again.'

He sat beside her and took her hand. 'How are you?' he asked quietly.

She shrugged. How was she? Strangely empty, considering she was about to get her heart's desire.

If only he could have greeted their forthcoming marriage and the prospect of their baby with happiness instead of a leaden duty. . .

'I'm all right,' she said eventually.

'I've spoken to Mr Maston — he sends his congratulations. We can get married this Friday if I get a licence on Tuesday morning. Luckily I'm not on duty.'

She nodded, unable to summon any enthusiasm for a hollow sham.

On his part, at least. Not on hers. She would mean her vows, every last one, and say them with conviction.

Gideon would obey them, but it would simply be another burden to shoulder, another responsibility to assume.

It was sad, when they could have had so much. . .

The plans for the wedding went ahead without a hitch. Beth went into town with Claire, intending to buy a simple little suit. She came home with a raw silk wedding dress in pale cream, smothered in seed pearls and tiny peach rosebuds, and bridesmaid's dresses for Claire and Sophie.

'You can't cheat us,' Claire had said, and Beth, unable to hurt them, went along with it. Gideon was paying — he had insisted and had given her what seemed like an extortionate amount of money.

They came home with very much less change than she had intended, and he just nodded and asked what she was doing about flowers.

'Oh — I hadn't thought of that.'

'I'll see the florist in the square,' Gideon told her. 'What do you want?'

She shrugged. 'Something simple.'

'OK. What about your parents?'

'What about them?' she asked, surprised.

'It's your wedding, Beth. Don't you want them here?'

She shook her head. 'No, I'll write to them. They won't be bothered.'

'What about friends?'

'Yes — there are some friends, about ten, I suppose. No relatives.'

'I need to know the numbers for the caterers,' he told her.

'Caterers?'

'For the reception,' he said patiently. 'The wedding's at twelve, so I thought a light buffet and everyone can get on their way before nightfall. It's New Year's Eve, too. I expect we'll have to put up quite a few here.'

'Oh.' She hadn't thought of the guests at all, or where they would stay or what they would eat. All she could think was the most wonderful thing in the world was about to happen to her, and she should feel something, surely! Something other than this dreadful emptiness. . .

She went into the house on the night before the wedding to ask Gideon if the flowers had arrived, and as she crossed the hall she heard him talking with his parents.

'I knew you were right for each other,' his mother was saying. 'Rupert, didn't I say that to you?'

'I expect so, dear,' his father said vaguely. 'Lovely girl, I thought — pretty as a picture and obviously thinks the world of you. I must say, if I had a pretty little slip of a thing like that chasing round after me I wouldn't hang about.'

'We haven't exactly hung about, Dad,' Gideon said with heavy irony. 'We've only known each other three and a half months.'

'It's enough,' his mother said calmly. 'With all that love on your side, what could possibly go wrong?'

Beth had her hand on the door knob when Gideon replied, and his words froze her in her tracks.

'I don't think love's got anything to do with it,' he said heavily, 'but never let it be said that I don't shoulder my obligations.'

She forgot what she had come for — forgot everything except the need to be alone with her pain.

She wanted to run, to pack her things and go away, but she couldn't. She wasn't like that.

In the morning she washed her hair and dried it, and was just putting on her make-up when Claire came running over.

'Do you need any help? Grannie said I should come and ask.'

Beth summoned a tiny smile. 'No, Claire, I'm fine. I've only got to put my dress on, and I can manage that. How about you and Sophie?'

'Grannie's helping us — are you sure you can cope?'

That was a different question altogether, but Beth pushed the smile a little further and sent Claire on her way.

At half-past eleven the church bells started to ring, and she heard the scrunch of gravel as Gideon's mother and father crossed the drive.

Gideon followed, with Claire and Sophie, looking beautiful in their matching ballerina-length pink silk dresses. Someone had put flowers in Sophie's hair, and Claire was walking with a grace and assurance that Beth had never seen in her before.

And Gideon — he looked magnificent in his hired morning suit, the cut emphasising the broad sweep of his shoulders — destined, she remembered with pain, to shoulder his obligations.

Just then he turned to speak to William, and his face looked carved in stone.

He glanced up at her, and her heart failed. He was grim-lipped and stern, and as their eyes locked, she knew she couldn't go through with it.

She couldn't! Not like this, an obligation to be shouldered! Throughout her childhood she'd been a burden on her parents, and she was damned if she and her baby were going to be a burden on anyone.

Straightening her shoulders, she turned away from the window and looked at her dress, still hanging on the front of the wardrobe.

No doubt the shop would take it back as it hadn't been worn. Otherwise she would pay for it — likewise the flowers, the caterers — oh, lord, there was so much, so many people here and she was going to let them all down. . .

No! She wouldn't let that stop her from doing the right thing. Gideon didn't want her. He'd told her months ago he had nothing left to give, and she should have listened then.

Except, of course, that even then she had been pregnant.

There was a tap on the door, and Will popped his head round.

'Beth? Can I come up?'

'Yes, do,' she said in a voice devoid of emotion.

He ran lightly up the stairs and came to a grinding halt in front of her. 'Beth — you aren't ready!'

'No.' Her hands twisted in the hem of her sweatshirt and she swallowed. 'Will, I want to talk to your father.'

'But he's gone into the church.'

'Please.'

Will looked helpless. 'But I can't just go in there and get him. Can I give him a message?'

'Yes — tell him I can't marry him.'

Will's jaw dropped. 'What! Beth, come on, what is this? Why not?'

'I'd rather tell Gideon, if you don't mind.'

He swore softly, then turned on his heel and ran down the stairs and out.

Moments later she heard a heavier tread on the iron steps and Gideon appeared.

His eyes scanned her, flicked to the dress on the wardrobe door and came back to her, empty.

'Beth?' he said. 'I thought—what is it?'

'All my life I've been a burden,' she told him quietly. 'You warned me a long time ago that you wouldn't marry me——'

'But this is different. You're——'

'No. It's no different. There are just more of us involved—more of a burden, more of a responsibility. Gideon, I can't do that to you, or to our baby. I won't have it brought up like I was, by resentful parents who feel trapped by its existence.'

'I won't resent the baby—what are you talking about?'

She laughed sadly. 'Maybe not the baby, then, but me—and I won't let myself be a burden again either. I need to belong, and if I can't——' She broke off, unable to continue.

'Beth—of course you'll belong! What are you talking about?'

'You don't want to marry me——'

'Of course I do!'

She shook her head. 'No—you don't. You're just shouldering your obligations, and I won't let you make that kind of sacrifice.'

'Shouldering my—Beth, you don't understand. Marriage is a responsibility, and I take my responsibilities seriously. I'm *afraid* to marry you, afraid I'll let you down, afraid I won't be able to give you what you deserve. But I'll do it, if that's what you want, because I love you, and I need you, and I'm not strong enough any more to turn you away.'

His eyes filled with tears, but he ignored them.

'Please think about it. I know you don't love me, but you thought you did once, and maybe with time — I know the kids can be real trial, but they love you, Beth, and I know they'd do anything for you — oh, God, darling, give us a chance, please? Give me a chance. . .'

She was still rooted to the spot, too stunned to move.

'Why didn't you tell me that you love me?' she whispered.

'Because I didn't know — or wouldn't admit it, anyway — until Will came into the church and told me that you wouldn't marry me. It hit me then, like a sledgehammer. I was just hiding from the truth, hiding behind my responsibilities so I didn't have to risk my heart, but it seems you'd stolen it anyway.'

He reached out his hand to her. 'Beth, please. . .'

Her heart overflowing, she threw herself into his arms and clung to him as he crushed her against his chest.

'I love you,' she whispered. 'Oh, darling — I thought you were just doing the decent thing, and I wanted so much to be loved. . .'

Her tears fell, soaking his shirt, and he laid his head down on hers and his tears mingled with her golden hair.

'So will you marry me?' he asked eventually.

'Of course I will.'

'Then — I don't want to hassle you, but we've got a church full of people waiting and unless you want to get married in jeans and trainers, you'd better get changed.'

She scrubbed her nose on the back of her hand, and

he gave her a large, pristine handkerchief. 'Blow your nose and sort out your make-up; I'll get the dress off the hanger.'

Her face was radiant, if a little streaky. She repaired the damage as fast as her shaking hands would allow, and then Gideon helped her into her dress.

'What about my hair? I was going to put it up ——'

'Leave it, there isn't time, and anyway I love it down.'

She brushed it out over her shoulders, pinned her veil on and slipped her feet into her shoes.

'How do I look?' she asked him nervously.

'Like a bride,' he said proudly, and grabbing her hand, he towed her down the steps and out on to the drive.

'Gideon, wait, I can't run on the gravel — oh!'

He scooped her up into his arms and carried her to the church, past the crowds who were waiting outside.

A huge cheer went up, and she turned her blushing face into his shoulder and laughed.

'Put me down! I refuse to be carried down the aisle like so much washing!'

He set her on her feet in the church, to the astonishment of the assembled guests, and straightened her veil.

'Thank God for that,' Will said fervently. 'Now get down there and wait for her, Dad.'

'One last thing,' he said, and turned to Beth. 'Just remember, every word I vow, I will mean with all my heart.'

Beth felt her tears overflow again, and a radiant smile broke out across her face.

'And mine, too,' she said softly.

Behind her Claire sighed. 'Well, isn't that the most romantic thing you ever heard!'

EPILOGUE

THERE was a splatter of gravel on the drive, and seconds later the door slammed.

'Dad!'

Feet pounded up the stairs, and as the door crashed back on its hinges, little Nicholas Pendragon sucked in a huge breath and bellowed furiously.

'I thought it was too good to last,' Gideon groaned, and opened his eyes.

'William — good morning.'

William, grinning from ear to ear, dangled a piece of paper over their noses.

Gideon snatched it, scanned the results and dropped back against the pillows. 'Thank God for that — we get rid of you.'

His grin widened. 'Oh, you would have done anyway, because if I hadn't got the grades for veterinary college I would have been a doctor.'

'A lesser qualification, of course,' Gideon said drily.

Beth slipped her legs over the side of the bed and went over to the crib standing by the fireplace.

'Did your nasty big brother wake you up, my darling?' she crooned softly, and lifted him into her arms. He turned towards her breast, his tiny rosebud mouth searching, and she smoothed the downy jet-black hair and smiled. 'Come and say well done to Will, then you can have breakfast.'

She walked over to her stepson and reached up to hug

him with her other arm. 'Congratulations—I knew you could do it. What did you get?'

'Four As, and ones in the biology and physics special papers.'

'Oh, clever-clogs. Well done.'

William reached down and stroked his little brother's cheek, and the baby instantly turned towards his finger. Frustrated to find no nipple there either, he let out another yell.

'He's hungry, let me feed him.'

Gideon threw back the bedclothes and propped up her pillows, and she climbed back on to the big bed beside him while William made himself comfortable on the end of the bed.

Seconds later there was a blissful silence.

'So, you really did it—well done,' Gideon said quietly to his oldest son. 'One down, three to go.'

Beth looked at the baby suckling noisily at her breast. 'Your Daddy's got plans for you, son. I should stay small, if I were you.'

Claire and Sophie came in then, Sophie with her rabbit, Claire rubbing her eyes and blinking blearily at the time.

'What's all the noise?' she asked sleepily.

Gideon lifted Sophie up and tucked her into the bed between them. 'Will's passed his A levels.'

Claire turned to him. 'Did you get good enough grades?'

William nodded, bursting with pride.

'Oh, great!' she shrieked, and flung her arms around her big brother. 'Oh, that's magic—can I have your room?'

Beside her Beth felt Gideon shake with laughter.

'What's funny, Daddy?' Sophie asked round her thumb.

'Nothing, Tuppence. Nothing at all. Life's absolutely perfect.'

'Or it would be if we could get a lie-in round here,' Beth murmured.

Nicholas had fallen asleep, his little mouth relaxed around her nipple, and Beth eased him away and handed him to Claire.

Very carefully, so as not to disturb him, she put her little brother back in his cot and covered him over. Then Will scooped Sophie out of the bed and carried her off, promising her all sort of wicked things for breakfast.

The door closed softly behind them, and Gideon drew Beth into his arms and snuggled her against his chest.

'I love you, Mrs Pendragon,' he said softly.

'I love you, too — but I think I might already have told you that.'

'Mmm — maybe, once or twice. I can't remember. When's your post-natal check?'

'Another week.'

'Is he really five weeks old?'

'Mmm. Doesn't it feel like it?'

Gideon laughed wryly. 'Oh, no — more like five months. I'm too old for this lark.'

'I hope not, because I'm just getting a taste for this.'

He groaned. 'Beth — can we talk about this in a sane moment?'

'When — about twenty years?'

'At least. Since I met you I've acquired a wife,

another child and two cats. Don't you think that's enough?'

She snuggled closer. 'It'll do — for now.'

'Thank God for that,' he said fervently, and stopped her smart reply with his lips.

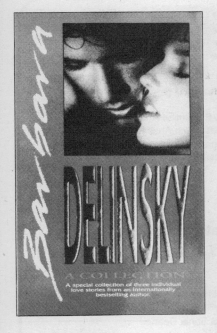

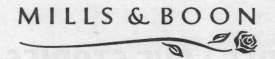

MILLS & BOON